The Counting of Sins

I0591602

Robert Joseph Greene

ISBN 13: 9780578787787

published by :

ICON EMPIRE PRESS

552 Church Street Toronto, ON

M4Y 2E3 CANADA.

NOTICE

All characters appearing in this work are fictitious in character. Any resemblance to any real persons, living or dead, is purely coincidental.

BOOK COVER ART

"Adam and Steve", 2017(digital media),
Artist : Michael Francis Flynn
Prints available via: **www.gayartshop.com**

ACKNOWLEDGMENTS

I would like to thank the New Jersey Historical Society,
the New Jersey Public Library Reference Department,
DignityUSA and Dignity Canada

CHAPTER ONE - TOM AND BAXTER

The frustrating sound of furniture being dragged on the floor and the sound of heavy objects bumping against the walls was one that Baxter hoped wouldn't be the welcoming sounds of his day. But they were, and his deep and beautiful sleep progressed into the brash reality of the noisy house. Yet as bad as it was, it wasn't the worst of his problems. Waking up that morning had also made him realize the truth of the fact that his mother was still dead. For below his bedroom, his mother was lying in state for viewing. Prior to that day, he felt self-assured that he was doing quite a good job on the part of removing the tragedy from his head. But now that he knew he would be seeing his dead mother lying in a coffin, it all started to come back. Right there in his bed, he had flashbacks to that day last week when he has come home from school to find his mother rambling incoherently and then she collapsed on the stairs. She never woke up.

As he dropped his feet from the bed to the cold floor, he cursed at himself for the cold that ran through his body, but also for the fact that he had woken up so late.

It wouldn't have been the case five days ago. His mother had always woken him and it was a luxury that he was going to miss.

Ironically, the cold in the room at the moment was a sharp contrast from the warm spring atmosphere that preceded the previous day. It was why he left the window open the night before. It was also why he could now hear the large crowd of people that had already come for the viewing just below his room.

"You don't know Dr. Holm? Why he's one of the most prominent doctors in New Jersey,"

or;

"She was originally Rose Smith from the Smith family of New York upper crust society before she married Holm. She was such a grand and elegant lady"

Baxter never imagined his mother's life before he came along. He wondered if she was happier before she married? He couldn't imagine his mother being happier than she was with him. Or even being happier with her husband, the prominent Doctor Holm of Newark. But his outlook on her happiness was one that he was going to have to discover by first understanding his own.

The voice of his neighbor interrupted his thoughts and brought him back into the reality of the day. Tom Harding was answering questions about the Holm family from the viewers who were waiting for the viewing to start. Tom was not only his neighbor but his classmate. Tom and Baxter were both eighteen years of age. Tom wasn't in the line-up of viewers but instead, he was bringing over a cake-loaf that his mother had baked for the Holm family.

As Baxter heard the distinct voice of his friend, he wished for a moment that Tom would come upstairs and give him a hug, but that was not how they engaged one another.

Tom's light jovial voice resonated so deeply into Baxter's essence that he got an unwanted erection.

It was the first time that a sexual thought had crawled into Baxter's mind about Tom. And he allowed it to remain there to fill the empty void from the absence of the normal occupying thoughts of his mother.

In order to get himself out of bed, he imagined his mother coming into his room and scolding him for staying in bed so late. It was a train of thought that worked remotely so he decided to continue the fantasy. He imagined her going into his closet and picking out his black Bergdorf Goodman suit, Brooks Brothers shirt and gold cufflinks from Tiffany Jewellers of New York.

Yet his imaginary guidance from his late mother was not enough to help him pick out the right bow tie. The bow ties were arranged neatly on his dresser and the large array of designs and patterns was one that further prompted his indecision. He was saved by remembering that it was proper to wear a bow tie for a funeral.

The fantasy dissipated when he thought of the funeral armband. It was his mother's funeral and she couldn't have possibly suggested that he wear it. But now he must.

To Baxter, his mother was the only person who loved him. Baxter knew that his father did not love him and he put no effort into pretending that he did.

When asked about his father, Baxter instinctively stated that he was a doctor and rarely mentioned the type of father that he was. But that was mostly because he actually didn't spend any time with his father. He knew that the man must have been a bad father owing to his unavailability, but he felt like he didn't exactly know who his father was as a person.

Baxter rolled over and placed the pillow over his head to drown out the noise. He had hoped that thoughts of Tom would enter into his head again.

CHAPTER TWO - THE FUNERAL

Tom wondered why his family wasn't able to attend the funeral church service for their neighbor, Mrs. Holm. The Hardings did, however, pay their condolences and were able to see Mrs. Holm lie in repose at the Holm's sprawling residence.

Tom remembered Mrs. Holm being such a radiant and cheerful person. She was always full of life but now she lied in state and the way she looked so solemn was something to marvel at. The veil that they placed over her while she lay in the dark oak coffin gave her once rosy complexion a darker grey hue and her outfit, a pink dress embroidered with flowers, was one that Tom did not remember seeing in the past, but it was beautiful all the same.

As the Holms had such a large following of acquaintances and friends, it was decided to extend the viewing over several days. The lines were usually long and often extended down the block over the course of these four days. This was due to the fact that it was a public viewing in the most prominent part of Newark, Forest Hills.

It was easy to ascertain who actually knew the Holms and who just came to see the elegant interior of their stately home that so few would ever normally see. Mrs. Holm sat on so many committees and boards for social and community services, it was easy to validate one's attendance just by a slight affiliation of some cause attributed to Mrs. Holm's volunteerism. The irony of it was that it wasn't quite as easy to ascertain the reason for Tom being there, although he had many reasons for being at the event.

Tom doesn't remember seeing Baxter there, but he did see Dr. Holm. The doctor was standing greeting those who passed by next to his sister-in-law, Grace. Grace had come to stay while the family got things in order. Mrs Holm's best friend Elizabeth Snavely, who was the wife of Dr. Earl H. Snavely, stood beside Grace as she would have known all the local attendees, thus helping Grace with the procession of viewers. Dr. Snavely was the medical director for Newark City Hospital and a close friend to Dr. Holm. The Snavely's were regular visitors to the Holm's residence and often the two families vacationed together.

Grace noticed that several dignitaries paid their respects including New Jersey Governor George Sestet, whose wife Henrietta was a good friend of Mrs. Holm. Former Newark Mayor Thomas Raymond and his wife Elizabeth also attended as well as Dr. Harrison Martland and his wife Myra. Dr. Martland would later become famous for coining the phrase, "punch drunk," with regards to brain injuries from the sport of boxing.

Dr. Holm looked so lost. It was as if his life was taken from him and not his wife. Tom thought no condolence would rest Dr Holm's grieving heart. His marriage to Mrs. Holm was his foundation and although he was Newark's most prominent physician, his wife was held in higher esteem as a New Jersey Socialite. As stated earlier, before she was married, she was Rose Smith from the prominent Smith family of New York. The society wives of Newark envied her wide connection to Manhattan social circles and for good reason.

But all this was gone, and the loss seemed greater to Dr. Holm than to anyone else including Baxter their only son. Dr. Holm was 20 years older than his wife and never would have imagined his beloved departing before him. So while he went through the process of grieving, he summoned whatever he could of his mental strength to constantly remind himself that he had to hold down what was left of his family, and that was his son, Baxter.

Tom Harding's family, on the other hand, though financially well off weren't as established but rather frowned upon by the Newark blue blood. They were

Anglo-papalists who were looked upon with suspicion by the older protestants of Newark Society. They attended Grace Church, whereas the most affluent of Newark society attended Trinity Church. Newark high society also had a strong anti-Catholic leaning and although Grace Church was Anglo-Papalist with no affiliation to the Roman Catholic Diocese, it was still considered "low brow" among the dominant protestant network in Newark. Both churches had Anglican roots. The Anglo-papalist movement came from the Oxford movement of 1833; Grace Church was comprised of people, beliefs and practices within Anglicanism that emphasized their Catholic heritage and identity of the various Anglican churches. However, any slight affiliation with Catholicism was despised by the other mainstream Anglicans.

The Hardings hated this stigma as Tom's family saw themselves as Anglo-Protestant like the rest of them and had no Irish Catholic affiliation whatsoever. Yet the burden was there, and it was felt more so by his mother who was often excluded from the tea parties and gala balls that she so badly wanted to attend.

Both families had stately homes right next to each other in the affluent Forest Hill district of Newark. Their large manicured lawns were the pride of the neighborhood. It was an affluent co-existence that often drove friendly gestures between the two families.

Mrs. Holm was cordial with the Harding family and every Christmas season, the Hardings were invited to the Holm's residence for drinks and merriment. However, the affluent co-existence had a twist of its own as the Hardings were only invited to certain functions that their wealth would only allow. The real Christmas party was always a private affair and the Hardings were aware that they weren't of the qualifying status afforded to the other wealthy circles to which the Holms affiliated. Every year, the Holms had a premier catered grand Christmas affair to which the Hardings were never invited. Tom's mother thought that it was because of their lack of status as Tom's father owned a successful delivery service. But the truth was that Mrs. Holm was more protective of the Hardings and didn't wish to expose them to the harsh criticisms of Newark's elite society. The Hardings just weren't in the right circles. While the Holms had a vacation home in the Hamptons, the Hardings summer home was in Long Shore New Jersey, which was considered a predominantly Jewish vacation spot. The Hardings had negro servants which was unheard of by the Newark elite. Mrs Holm was also embarrassed by the hypocrisy of her inner women's circle. Lois Clancy was the first of their blue blood circle to employ a negro cook which the other ladies thought to be progressive.

Notwithstanding, Mrs. Holm truly cherished what little friendship she had with Mrs. Harding. She saw Mrs. Harding as a truly pure warm breeze of fresh air compared to the stale, aloof, and mean spirited entitled tippling wives of the other established families. This was something that continually grew their budding friendship before the unfortunate death.

The only time the Hardings could get a glimmer of the upper crust of Newark was during Baxter's birthday party as most of the prominent families attended. Yet, Tom couldn't understand why Baxter wasn't allowed to attend any of his birthday parties. Despite their family differences, a friendship grew and although he never attended Tom's parties, Baxter would always present an expensive and exquisite birthday gift to which Tom always cherished. When they were younger, the gifts often came from FAO Schwarz or some other high-end Manhattan retailer. As they grew, the gifts might have differed greatly, but the gesture remained and that was pretty much all that was needed to keep the fire of their friendship burning.

Tom was a sportsman. He loved stick ball and football. He played for Newark Academy, his high school team, and hoped to attend Columbia University when he graduated. He was full-bodied, masculine and clean cut. Baxter, on the other hand, was tall, slender and more bookish. Baxter had masculine features but was neither sporty nor outgoing. It was a yin-yang relationship and a suitable contrast in personalities that withstood the strongest tests of friendship.

After the death, Baxter's world had significantly changed. He was torn from the loving protective arms of his mother too early and the father that he was left with was not making matters any better at all. Dr Holms was a Yale graduate and a board member of the Skull and Key Society, which later became the Theta Nu Epsilon fraternity. It was the perfect platform for Dr. Holm to help his son get into Yale. But Dr. Holm steered Baxter away from any hopes of going there for reasons that Baxter believed had to do with his father's disapproval of him.

It wasn't Baxter's looks or intelligence that Dr Holm disliked in his son but rather his passive, bookish mannerisms. Holm's only hope was that a strong-willed woman would pull Baxter right and make him an outstanding member of society, which hadn't materialized through his mother's upbringing.

Mrs. Holm doted and smothered Baxter as she didn't want to share him with any other which was why he became shy and awkward with others. Baxter was polite, positive, and could carry a conversation but preferred to keep his company to himself or be alone with his mother. He always yearned for her approval and she gave it freely and willingly, what they had not realized at the time was that he would grow to become too accustomed to this approval. That he would not live his life to the tune of what impressed society. And while that can be a good thing sometimes, it can be a basic necessity to get by the primary aspects of living. Especially because Dr. Holm was a primary citizen.

Dr. Holm wasn't jealous as he had no real relationship with his son when compared to Baxter's mother, but rather he worried about his son's future being influenced by such an overbearing mother.

Tom saw all of this from what little exposure he had to the Holm's household and he tried his best to get Baxter to come out of his shell. To the disappointment of the other boys in the neighbourhood, Tom would often include Baxter when they went fishing or bobsledding. It was a inconvenience the other boys would have to deal with if they were to enjoy the team spirit that Tom brought. Baxter never wanted to disappoint Tom and would go along, but was squeamish with worms or too worried he'd get hurt bobsledding. Baxter would faithfully wait on the sidelines while the other boys enjoyed themselves and while this often worried Tom, it was sufficient enough that he was there.

*

With the last viewer attended to, Dr. Holm was glad to see the front doors locked and the procession of faces come to a close. He retired into his office for solace but solace didn't come. The loss of his wife made him doubt himself for the first time. He wondered how he could he go on living without her. Their years together meant the world to him as she helped him in ways no other could imagine. Rose was a very well-bred caring and loving person.

He questioned his decision to turn over care for her illness to specialists and not care for her himself. However, Mrs. Holm's illness and death came on so suddenly that he was certain that he would not have been able to save her anyway.

This made it especially difficult for the doctor as he tried to his fullest abilities to remember any major disagreement between them and he could not. He even searched as far back as to their first years of marriage and again could only remember the joys of growing together.

Dr. Holm's medical training, military training, and personal development focused on one clear aspect of his personality that he now regrets. His composure. Dr. Holm was trained and taught to never fault, to never cry alone in his study. And yet, this was what he wanted so desperately but couldn't bring himself to do.

His mind was caught in a conundrum of all his training as a doctor and as a man to hold himself together in times of crisis, but on the other hand, he needed to cry to express his loss of love. This stressed him more than anything else.

Did he not love his wife?

This wasn't even a question in his mind. He loved her more than life itself, which was why he questioned the reason to go on living.

Had he been his younger self, he would have drowned his sorrows in whiskey but this was in the time of prohibition and the doctor kept such little alcohol at his residence that he doubted that he had enough liquor around to make him drunk.

He wallowed in the widening abyss between the love of his wife and the sorrow from losing her.

Yes, Dr. Holms would have given anything to cry for his loss. He concluded that crying was the luxury of artisans and not for men of his stature. He loathed the freedom one has in the artist's world that is lost to his kind.

His mind then turned to anger as the loss of his wife brought upon a question of fairness in a world that he found increasingly cruel.

What did he have left? A profession which he blindly followed by the traditions of his family? A son that he didn't really know nor cared for in a way that he saw in other fathers? The house and summer homes that Rose decorated to her taste which would now be a constant reminder of his loss?

As a doctor, when given a challenging medical case, he had so many doctors to consult with for answers, but for the death of his own wife, he knew of no one to turn to. Even inviting his wife's sister to stay brought him no calmness for his grieving soul. Grace wasn't as charming and beautiful as her sister. Grace was outgoing and a bit of a bavard with no real topic of interest except gossip.

Dr. Holms lamented over the death of his wife for hours in his study. The sun had long set when the parlour maid informed him that dinner was ready. Knowing that Rose planned the meals, he asked what was prepared. The maid said that Grace had instructed a meal of roast beef and carrots and but even then he dismissed her saying that he wasn't hungry for anything.

Grace was the unsung hero of the moment. She had taken the spot over which her sister would normally triumph. When their parents died, it was Rose who followed protocol and arranged all that was necessary for a successful funeral. Grace was in such awe of her sister's abilities in times of need.

Much to her parent's chagrin, Grace had married a minister of an Episcopal Church and relocated far up the Hudson Valley, close to Albany, New York. They had a childless marriage and Grace had confessed to her sister that she had wished she followed her parent's advice and married into a well-established family.

Grace missed the long telephone conversations where Rose would give details of grand New York Gala balls or prominent receptions that she and the doctor attended.

Grace loved how at the end of each "season", she would get her sister's discarded dresses and gowns but never did she get jewelry. Grace lacked the necessary accessories like jewelry to go with such outfits as her husband the reverend found jewelry to be too ostentatious and felt it would set a bad example to his followers. So, Grace was left with only a partial display of wealth that she once knew as a young girl.

Grace wasn't given a budget to arrange any of the provisions for the celebration of the life of her sister and she spent lavishly. She thought that someone would have said something if they felt it wasn't proper, but the reality was that Grace was long out of touch with high society and her expenses were in line with the current social order of Newark's elite.

A few moments later, Grace knocked at the doctor's private home office door. She had come to remind Holm's that protocol stipulated that a meal be served for out of town family and that he should attend.

Since the majority of family members were his in-laws, which he didn't care for, Dr. Holm declined to attend the dinner. Grace being the gregarious person that she was would have normally impressed upon the doctor the importance of making an appearance to his extended family, but she decided that it would be best to let the doctor have a moment to himself. She was feeling the brunt of the loss of her sister as well and the last thing she wanted was to try and force the man out of his shell. He typically did not associate with them prior to the loss, so she didn't expect that he would now.

But keeping Rose's memory alive meant doing the things that she would have done and standing for the things that she would have stood for. So she knew deep down that she had to take care of Dr. Holmes and Baxter. She didn't want the responsibility, but they were family. In times like these, family was all that mattered.

CHAPTER THREE - THE PROPOSITION

With the funeral behind them Baxter and Tom went back to being their old selves again. As Baxter was an only child, his only outlet for anything remotely close to being siblings were the Harding boys: Tom and William.

Tom was your all American boy. He was witty, athletic and handsome. William was the younger of the two and had all the characteristics of his brother, which made them, at times, rivals instead of brothers.

Baxter always played the role of mediator when the two brothers got into arguments or fights. The Harding boys appreciated the fair minded gentle approach Baxter brought to settling disputes. Baxter appreciated his position with the boys as he liked feeling needed. If he were to confess anything it was that he had a slight preference for Tom over William. However, it was never noticed in settling matters between the two brothers.

Baxter and Tom often walked home together from school on Market street often stopping at Sedwick's for a fountain soda then catching the trolley which, stopped on the outskirts of Forest Hill. However, when Tom had sporting events, Baxter walked home alone.

On this particular day, some hooligans cornered Baxter and accosted him when he refused to give them money. They took his leather wallet, belt and shoes. Baxter came home bloodied and crying. Dr Holm dressed his son's wounds but made no comforting effort to console his son other than telling him to go rest in his room. Dr. Holm thought it foolish for an 18 year old man to cry, but said nothing.

Baxter was not the son that he had hoped for. Dr. Holm, being a self made man, had hoped that, by 18 years of age, his son would have grown into his own. It wasn't that Baxter was unintelligent, meagre in stature, or even had any fault to show as a disability except one.

Baxter was terribly shy. The doctor observed his son as being clever enough to avoid discussion with his contemporaries even when he knew the subject matter. Baxter was content with being looked over or disappearing into a crowd at functions.

Dr. Holms hated that nothing really stood out about his son that he could comment positively upon to others.

When Baxter was gone. Dr. Holm closed the door to his office and wrote a note for Tom to come over immediately.

Tom had just entered his home when he saw the Holm's parlour maid give a note to their cook, Mabel. She stopped the moment she saw him.

"There he is" she said, "young man, I have a note from Dr. Holm for you."

Mabel was standing behind her and held out her hand with the sealed note.

"I think you need to come right away. It has something to do with Baxter."

A tinge of nervousness shot through Tom's spine. He was about to leave when Mabel suggested that he wash up before going over to Dr. Holm's office.

Tom dropped his books in his room and went to the washroom to freshen up.

By the time he returned, the parlour maid was gone. Tom proceeded to run along the side of his house, through the yard and jump over the adjoining bush. This was all noticed from Dr. Holm through his large office window. Tom bowed his head as if to greet Dr. Holm not knowing if Dr. Holm disapproved of him not using the walkway. However he did walk up to the front door and ring the bell.

The same parlour maid opened the door with a smile on her face.

"Young Tom, go right in he's waiting for you."

Tom knocked on Dr. Holm's office door.

"Come in Tom." Dr. Holm said in a not so loud but assertive voice.

When Tom opened the door, he saw Dr. Holm was still looking out the window. He turned and offered Tom a seat at a side table to the right of his enormous mahogany desk. Tom took the seat closest to him and Dr. Holm sat in the adjoining seat.

"I'm so glad you could come Tom. I heard that you were at football practice."

Tom always felt uncomfortable talking to adults but usually no one noticed by the way he spoke. He seemed both positive and assertive.

"Yes, sir, I hope to play college football." Tom replied.

"Rumor has it that a scout from Rutgers College called upon you at home."

Tom wondered how Dr. Holm knew this but remembered that Baxter was present when the man arrived from Rutgers College to interview him.

"You know West Point has a wonderful football team. It's my alma mater. I can put in a good word for you with our state senator to get you in if you'd like."

Tom thanked Dr. Holm but confessed that he had his heart set on Columbia University.

"Columbia? Why their football team is nothing but an upstart." Dr. Holm said despairingly.

Although Dr. Holm seemed confrontational, he enjoyed this banter and wished that this were the type of conversation he could have with his own son. Tom knew the right words to say to Dr. Holm to turn the conversation in his favour.

"Yes, but although my heart is set on Columbia, I hope to follow in your footsteps by going into medicine." Dr. Holm looked upon the young boy with pride.

"If you can keep a secret, I have a little apricot wine stashed away, would you like some?"

It was the height of the prohibition, but Tom was no stranger to drinking. Tom's hesitancy was due to the fact that both his mother and grandmother were strong temperance lobbyists. His great grandmother was a founding member of the temperance movement in Newark.

Dr. Holm knew that the Hardings ran a dry house, but he also knew this would be a good bonding ice breaker as Dr. Holm never had the opportunity to have a sit down with the young lad.

"It will be our secret," Dr. Holm added while making a humorous pointing gesture towards the Harding's home.

Tom nodded in acceptance and soon Dr Holm got up from his chair and went to his office credenza and brought out an elaborate decanter with matching miniature cups. He poured each a glass and sat down.

"Look Tom, I'll get right to the point."

Dr. Holm went on to explain the incident that happened to Baxter earlier that day which made Tom feel guilty and sad for not being there for his friend.

Tom's mind drifted as Dr. Holm spoke.

"Which is why I'm offering this proposition to you," were the last words Tom caught from Dr. Holm's conversation.

Tom was offered two dollars per session to give boxing lessons to Baxter. This came as a complete surprise, and this seemed quite a lot of money to Tom.

There was a condition attached to it, and that was he was never to mention this to Baxter's Aunt Grace. Dr. Holm said that Grace wasn't a fan of pugilism but the reality was that she didn't approve of Dr Holm trying to make Baxter into something he was not.

Dr. Holm shared his disappointment about his son with Grace and he didn't like how Grace almost instinctively felt a need to protect Baxter from Dr. Holm's harsh judgements. However, the feelings ran deeper in Dr. Holm as he knew that his beloved wife would have felt the same way and he would have dared not attempt such an offer had his wife been alive.

A tinge of nostalgia and pain came over Dr. Holm at the thought of his dear late spouse.

Tom wondered if Baxter knew about this offer and why he wasn't present when this proposal was offered. But, in actuality, Baxter was there, quietly listening in the hallway.

"Tom, I don't want you to go easy on him."

"Excuse me?"

"You know how Baxter is. I know what the other boys say about him"

"He's swell," Tom said in a defensive manner as would any good friend say.

"No, he's passive and quiet. He needs to be more assertive. If you haven't figured it out, I'm paying you to make a man out of him. Do you understand?"

Without giving Tom a chance to answer, Dr. Holm went to the door to call his son. His heavy footsteps gave Baxter a chance to escape unnoticed.

Baxter appeared somewhat solemn before his father.

"Come, I have Tom here for you. We have a surprise."

Baxter entered and Tom stood up. Tom felt cornered and knew that Baxter wouldn't be happy with his father's proposal. Dr. Holm told the boys to sit.

"Son, I asked Tom here to help you mature. Tom is so great at sports and you need to expand interests. This is why I told Tom to teach you boxing."

Baxter was thoroughly embarrassed by the conversation and knew where this was heading. It was the first time, since his mother's death, that his father addressed him directly. Baxter had hoped that this discussion would be in private but his father laid out the truth about his son, albeit through suggestion and not via judgement.

"But I don't like to fight."

"Well, I think in light of today's episode, it's necessary. You have to learn to defend yourself."

"There were four boys, dad, and I was just one."

"I'm sure that Tom would have put up a good fight against them, but you, I don't know."

Dr. Holm looked at Tom and smiled.

"I believe that Tom would have faired better in this situation or at least with enough bravado to have scared them off."

Baxter felt humiliated and embarrassed by his father's words. He wanted to run from the room but knew that would have fed into his father's perception of him.

Tom was equally embarrassed by Dr. Holm's unkind words towards his only child.

When the proposal was done and set into motion, Dr. Holm concluded the meeting with a firm handshake for both of them.

Baxter left without even a word to Tom. Dr. Holm escorted the young man to the door and apologized for his son's lack of social grace.

CHAPTER FOUR - THE FIGHT

Baxter avoided Tom for the rest of the week. When the day came for his first boxing session, he came into Tom's yard and called out to his window. He didn't go into the house. He was wearing Gym shorts and an undershirt. Baxter was surprised to see Tom come out in a blazer and slacks.

"I know you don't have any gloves and I don't have a spare. So, I thought we'd go downtown to Koenings and get you some gloves for your first lesson."

Baxter was relieved by the offer and hurried back home to change.

They took the Hardings car which was a Pierce - Arrow. It was an older model compared to the Holm's brand-new apple green Packard Town car and wasn't a limousine but still none the less it was a highly esteemed car. Baxter hated the color as he thought it too puerile for a car of such stature.

While driving Tom confessed that Dr. Holm sprung this on him and vowed to make this training as painless as possible.

Baxter was relieved by Tom's gesture. Then Baxter pierced the level of civility between them.

"Tom, I'm going to be frank with you, I love my father but I don't necessarily like him."

Tom was shocked by this confession. He thought it was a rather obstinate and unchristian statement.

"How could you say that, look at all the things your father has provided for you."

"No, Tom, you don't understand, my father would say the same thing about me."

Tom was uncomfortable with this conversation and quickly changed the subject. Tom thought briefly about his own father. He would have never made such a statement. His father was proud of him, loving, and caring.

Tom wasn't mature enough to see the difference in the two father's characters to form such a basis of understanding from Baxter's point of view.

For Tom, his parents were always right and children were always wrong. He never had to question such things in his own life.

It was at that moment that Tom felt concerned about Baxter's unhappiness. It was a realization brought upon him by these statements from Baxter. He had always thought Baxter to be melancholic but now, for the first time, understood the foundations from where it came.

He was glad to have arrived at the sporting goods store only because it allowed him to easily change the subject.

E.G. Koening & Sons was the largest sporting goods store in Newark. It came about due to the high demand for sporting goods from the surrounding Rutgers College and sporting clubs. Baxter actually laid aside his trepidation of sports and actually found the act of trying on the various gloves rather enjoyable in Tom's company.

Upon payment, Tom noticed a flyer looking for boxing enthusiasts for an Amateur Boxing event being held at the Lyric Theatre. The purse was set at five dollars. Tom thought he should apply.

"Why would you want to sign up for that?" Baxter asked.

"I don't know. It sounds exciting."

"There can't be anything even remotely thrilling about being pummelled by your opponent." Baxter retorted.

"Well, if you're doing the pummelling you don't have to worry about that sport."

Baxter loved how Tom always had a positive upside to everything.

Tom and Baxter went to the Athletic club, as mentioned in the flyer, to enlist Tom for the amateur event.

Tom spent weeks preparing for this event. When he wasn't at after school football practice or helping Baxter, Tom was practicing for the match at the Newark Athletic Club. His knuckles were bruised from hitting the canvas punching bag, suspended on thick chains anchored from the ceiling. Baxter proved useful as he was good at holding the punching bag for Tom to hammer it with jabs and punches.

The Lyric Theatre Boxing Club on Market street often hosted late night weekend boxing or wrestling matches on alternative weeks. The theatre didn't seem to fit the standard layout for boxing matches like at the Olympic A. It was a theatrical theatre which lacked the encompassing circular seating around a rink like traditional boxing establishments. Although it had a nicely decorated theatre with art nouveau decor, tonight it smelled of sweat, cigar smoke and illegal booze. However, the cops turned a blind eye having received discreet financial payments from the bookies. Tom was in the pregame show where amateur boxing matches were displayed before the Big Match. The major event that evening was a well-known local negro boxer named Young Siki and a white boxer named Clive Wills. Clive Wills was very well known in boxing circles and had been successful in the boxing circuit throughout New York, New Jersey and Pennsylvania. Clive had your typical boxer look with the heavy brow ridge, boxer's pug nose and large v-shaped brick house physique. He was considered the favorite among the bookies as he worked with them to fix his fights.

If the bookies want Clive to knock out his opponent in round four, Clive made certain that it happened. The kickbacks to Clive for this loyalty were substantial, often four times the amount of the purse.

The sound of leather hitting skin is a unique sound blurred out only by the lively crowd in attendance in the Theatre. The oily thud heard over and over again as boxing gloves hit skin seemed to invigorate this crowd of mainly younger flappers and older working-class men from around the area.

The night of the match sent an adrenaline rush through Tom's body that he hadn't felt before.

Tom sat in one corner of the stage while his opponent sat on the other. The referee pulled each contestant forward as he announced them. When it was his opponents turn to be announced, the crowd seem to applaud more in his favour.

With the ring of the bell, the fighting commenced.

Tom dodged the first swing from his opponent, a Jewish guy from the Third Ward named Samuel. Tom remembered from his days at Sunday school, when he was younger, that Samuel meant "God has heard" in Hebrew.

Samuel was short, very compact, and fit. He was agile which Tom wasn't; however the thrusts of his opponent's punches were weak whereas Tom had a formidable jab that repeatedly knocked the opponent off balance but didn't topple him.

One particular punch given by Tom almost made Samuel fall which made the crowd yell and jump in anticipation but he got up quickly. The sudden loud Roar of the crowd attracted Clive's attention.

Clive had a tendency to sit and watch the amateur match before his big fight. It tended to give him the much-needed adrenaline rush for his matches. As he scanned the crowd his eyes fell on Baxter. Baxter seemed over dressed and too nicely polished to be in a crowd of hooligans and working class men which was the typical audience. Clive saw a feminine charm in the young man, which he had rarely seen in this crowd. It was obvious that Baxter was uncomfortable watching the fight and he wondered why he even stayed.

It was clear Samuel's strategy was to maneuver about the rink to tire Tom but he under-estimated Tom's stamina and endurance. Tom caught on early that Samuel routinely feigned with his right and then swung a left jab.

Samuel realized, after some failed blocks on his part and a few good face blows, he was losing focus. Samuel began to embrace Tom more thus buying time to re-position while the referee broke them up.

Over time, the crowd realized that Samuel didn't have an alternative strategy and they were thirsty for a knockout.

Tom was absolutely focused and determined to win. Ten minutes into the fight he knew this was going to be a difficult match.

It was one thing for Baxter to practice boxing, but it was another thing to actually witness a live match. It is especially difficult if it's your best friend in a boxing match and you don't want him to get hurt. Baxter felt sick to his stomach from nerves. You could tell that the crowd quickly identified Tom as the better boxer. Tom was giving one hundred and ten percent in this fight as if his manhood was at stake.

Samuel had surpassed everyone's expectations for lasting as long as he did. But Samuel was tiring and getting sloppy. By the fifth round, the crowd was hungry for blood. The noise levels were deafening, and it was hard to concentrate. It's no surprise that both boxers qualified for the amateur's match because they both were the strongest boxers from the selection of applicants. Even so, only one man was going home with the five dollar purse win and Baxter hoped it was Tom.

A guy behind Baxter shouted out Tom's name and got the rest of the crowd to follow suit. It really angered Baxter that he couldn't bring himself to shout out Tom's name for fear of calling unwanted attention upon himself. He pondered this for a moment and wondered if he was being too paranoid. He heard other guys shout out his friend's name from the rows behind him. Why couldn't he?

Samuel was pretty good at blocking most of Tom's punches to the face for most of the match, but he was tired.

With only five seconds left on the clock for round seven, Samuel succumbed to his fatigue and went down on a direct hit to the face.

The hysterical crowd spilled out from behind, overcoming Baxter in his seat, as the referee did the count calling the match in Tom's favour. Even Clive was caught up in the excitement.

Clive saw that Tom was looking for someone in the crowd until Tom's eye's laid upon Baxter. He knew then that Baxter and Tom were friends.

Clive went back to the locker room/waiting area but Baxter's face was burned into his memory. He was hoping that he'd stay for his match.

Clive's match was the main event and the crowd was completely energized from the previous amateur match. It was actually a short match to which Clive annihilated his opponent within five rounds as instructed. The purse win was twenty dollars which was a sizeable amount in those days.

It was well into two in the morning when Clive exited the boxing club. When he was outside he saw Tom and Baxter talking to a young couple about a speakeasy not far from downtown. They were walking towards a new and very expensive Packard town car. Baxter entered into the driver's seat. Tom was the passenger.

Clive pondered whether to go to the speakeasy or go and drink his mickey of whisky alone in the park before he went home.

Speakeasies were fairly new, and you could only find them via word of mouth.

Melinda's Alley was probably the most popular speakeasy in Newark. It was located in an alleyway near the Central Railroad Station warehouse district. In fact, the speakeasy was in the basement of a produce warehouse.

It had a huge mirror from the old defunct Albemarle Hotel from Manhattan, a large bar without stools and lots of small tables and chairs for customers.

Melinda, although pretty, seemed like she had seen life at its worse. She was a no non-sense gal but fair. It was rumoured that she was the lover of famed bootlegger Joseph 'Doc' Rosen.

A buzzer announced the arrival of potential guests. Melinda would look them over through a window peep hole and give the okay for the doorman to let them in. If she didn't know them well, then they wouldn't get in. However, those in the know, knew to wave to her from the window and hold up a dollar. This was the bribe to get in.

Liquor or booze often was made in the cellar, blended with the imported stuff, then placed back into the brand named bottles. Everyone knew this but didn't complain. It was prohibition and they had nowhere else to go.

It was extremely smokey and crowded by the time Baxter and Tom arrived. They were both nervous. They had never been to a speakeasy before. It was a relief to be inside at last. The boys found an abandoned table in back that still had dirty glasses on it.

An all negro jazz band was playing in front of them with a big boned yet attractive well-dressed negress singing an upbeat jazzy song. People were tapping to the music, but dancing wasn't allowed.

The barmaid came and cleared the glasses. She quickly returned ready with her pad, gazing at herself in the mirror while the boys studied the menu.

"Whiskey…Bourbon?" Tom said while looking at Baxter for approval.

Baxter just nodded nervously.

The waitress disappeared and came back moments later, with two mismatched glasses of booze with a single ice cube in each. Tom paid her immediately and she disappeared again without even saying thank you.

Tom tried to make a joke with Baxter, who seemed overwhelmed by the surroundings.

"So, you come here often?"

To which Baxter wrinkled his brow and smiled.

Baxter was quick to get the next round of drinks and pay to show Tom that he wouldn't let him loose his winnings on him.

By the third drink, they were both sufficiently inebriated.

Their world was now a dizzying slurry of sound and blurred lights. They swayed to the music. A real jezebel in a satin party dress and too much makeup approached the young men. She was equally as drunk and had a martini glass in her hand but seemed to be spilling it everywhere.

"You look like my little brother" she slurred leaning rather closely into Tom until she lost her balance and fell into his lap.

Tom laughed but was shocked by the forward gesture. Until now, he only heard of swinging flappers but to see one in action was quite exciting for him.

All the girls that they knew were prim and proper.

Her voice chimed and blended with the distant sound of the jazz music and clicking heels.

"Excuse me?" Tom said unable to hear her. So she leaned into his face.

"I said you look like my little brother."

All three laughed hysterically.

"I'm Penelope but people call me Peachie, " she said while ruffling Tom's hair.

Baxter felt a tinge of jealousy but was very polite.

"Hi Peachie, I'm Baxter and this is Tom."

Baxter's gesture of a handshake made her giggle. She didn't oblige but instead took a sip of her drink and nodded.

Tom was enthralled by the attention.

Peachie suddenly changed her mind and went to extend her hand to Baxter but lost her balance, spilling a sizeable amount of her drink onto Tom's lap.

Miraculously, the waitress came with a towel, handing it to Peachie who instinctively blotted out the dampness on Tom's pants.

Tom was becoming visibly erect which made him feel embarrassed.

Peachie laughed while looking at Tom's crotch.

"Did I do that?" she said flirtatiously.

Baxter really didn't like Peachie and grew tired of the whole scene. He told Tom that he wanted to go and that it was late. Tom seemed disappointed but followed Baxter as he got up to leave.

"Hey!" Peachie pouted, "buy me a drink."

Baxter turned to her and said that they would after they come back from the men's room but they never returned.

Baxter was silent in the car which he shouldn't have been driving as he was very drunk.

"Where are we going?" Tom asked.

Baxter turned into Branch Brook Park. It was known as the "lover's lane" of Newark. He pulled the enormous car into a shady area and parked.

"I have to relieve myself."

He got out of the car and walked towards the back of the car to pee. Tom soon followed him but kept his distance to pee, too.

"What did you have against Peachie? She seemed swell." Tom asked while peeing.

Baxter, annoyed by the question, pondered the best response he could muster being drunk.

"I felt she was going to use us to get free drinks." He coldly retorted.

Tom went on to explain that it would have been okay since he had his purse winnings. This unnerved Baxter, who returned to the car. As he walked towards the drivers side he heard Tom say that he was going to be sick.

Tom vomited extending his hand to the car for balance. He took out his handkerchief and cleaned his face and returned to the passenger side of the car.

Tom was breathing heavily and sweat had appeared on his brow. He turned to look at Baxter but had trouble focusing.

Baxter looked back but then leaned in and kissed Tom passionately.

Tom meant to resist but was too drunk to do so.

Tom's passivity made Baxter think that he wanted this to happen too. He was excited, extremely curious and wanted to see what Tom's penis looked like. He tried to undo Tom's pants to pull it out but it was impossible in the cramped front seat.

Baxter lifted Tom's hips up off the seat, opened his belt, and shoved his pants and underpants down revealing his genitals.

To Baxter, Tom's erect penis was the most beautiful thing he'd ever seen. It was pink, long, and girthy. Though he had no way of judging other than his own. He knew that Tom's was bigger than his.

Baxter at first licked Tom's penis. It was watery and a little slimy from the sweat, and salty but he continued.

Baxter slipped Tom's penis into his mouth. Tom began thrusting a little. Baxter strained to make sure his teeth didn't scratch Tom's skin but the size of his penis made it difficult. He also wasn't experienced with the art of giving fellatios. Neither of them were.

Baxter knew this was wrong but enjoyed feeling it in his mouth. Above him he heard sounds of Tom's moans. When Tom ejaculated, Baxter pulled away. Some of Tom's cum hit his face. It was extremely hot to the touch. The rest splattered back onto Tom.

Baxter gave Tom his handkerchief.

"Sorry" was all Baxter could say.

They drove in complete silence. Even when Baxter parked, Tom just got out without saying "goodbye" and went home. The lightness of day was upon them but the sun hadn't risen just yet.

As he crawled into bed, Baxter cried himself to sleep feeling that he lost his only friend.

Later that morning, Tom woke up feeling nauseous and hungover. He remained in bed trying to piece together the events of last night.

The knock on the door by his mother felt like hammer shots to his head.

"Tom, why aren't you ready for church?"

His mother pleaded with him to go to church but he resisted. She left to ask Tom's father to intervene.

Mr. Harding wasn't as stern. Tom promised to go to evening services which seemed to appease both his parents. Mr. Harding, suspecting Tom's condition, told him to rest and drink lots of water.

His only words to his son were: "I hope this doesn't become a habit son. This is the wrong road you'd be taking in life."

Tom assured his father that this was a mistake and would never happen again. He then went back to sleep.

Tom never imagined intimacy with a man before and even in his thoughts of women it was more of an imagery of nudity as he had no idea about sex, which he left to learn about when married.

However, the thrill of the physical contact and the resulting ejaculation was far too impactful for him to forget.

Tom had to fight his thoughts all day as Baxter dominated every corner of his mind. There was a new feeling that he was experiencing and he didn't understand

47

it. However, he knew it was wrong and that he had to suppress it.

At night, Tom even started to dream about Baxter. The dreams weren't sexual but they were intimate. They were walking on the beach holding hands or on a blanket in the park cuddling.

Tom was getting more confused about what had happened and needed help. He felt the best thing to do was to get spiritual guidance.

Tom was taught that it was through confessions that one released the burdens of daily sins before God to warrant forgiveness through penitence. This was how Tom was raised but never before had he had a confession that would bring such shame before his reverend.

Tom walked around nervously as he watched the other parishioners enter the church for the evening Sunday service. He somehow feared going into the church for he was too ashamed of himself. Although the thought of blame didn't apply to Baxter in particular but rather the entire chain of events from last night.

He decided to wait until the evening church service had ended and evening confessions began for it to be the most opportune moment to enter.

The confessional was situated in the side of the narthex, almost completely apart from the main hall.

When it was his turn to enter the confessional, he winced to himself in anticipation for what he was about to reveal.

Tom was a local celebrity to his congregation. As his local high school football success was their pride and joy.

Tom kneeled and look towards the screen viewing cut out which slid open revealing a vague image of Reverend Gomph seated on the other side.

"Bless me father for I have sinned. It has been seven days since my last confession, and these are my sins. I have used the Lord's name in vain on at least four occasions. I have engaged in drinking, but more important, I got drunk. And from this, I have indulged in pleasures of the flesh. A pleasure so unholy that I feel sick to my stomach."

"The basic requirement for a good confession my son is to have the intention of returning to God"

"Yes father, and I want so badly to return to God."

"You are young and pleasures of the flesh are so enticing to you, but you must remember who stands with you. God stands with you and he sees all."

At that moment, Tom started to cry.

"Father, it's so bad. It was so carnal. It was not with a girl."

"Ah," said Father Gomph as he paused to think of the right words to say.

"Son, I know you so hear my comforting words. You are a great servant of God. I know all the good deeds you have done. You are a great athlete, a great son and are about to become a man but have you counted the sins in your life until now?"

"Yes, father I have."

"Then you know of God's limit for forgiveness."

"Yes, father I do."

"Okay, for your penance I shall ask you to do fifty our Father and fifty Hail Marys and go to pray if ever you have this urge for carnal pleasure again."

"Thank you father."

In the end, Tom's soul was not as resolved as he had hoped.

CHAPTER FIVE - THE TIME APART

For the next couple of weeks Tom avoided Baxter. He didn't walk with him after school nor did they meet for practice. When Dr. Holm sent money for Baxter's boxing lesson, he gave it back to the parlour maid with a note explaining that his football practice schedule had changed and that he would not be able to help Baxter.

Baxter, also avoided Tom but not for the same reasons. Baxter feared Tom's rejection. The episode in the car was all his fault. He felt that Tom would judge him. Baxter felt worthless and withdrew even further into self-isolation.

Tom seem to take a different approach. Since their episode in the car, he began to socialize more. He, along with some other football team members, were invited to a garden party hosted by the Summerville's. It was the first party of the summer season. Tom didn't know Margaret Summerville well but she had graduated from Central High School. She was Bud Cronheim's cousin. Bud was a teammate and invited Tom, Chad, and Ellis to her party as Margaret wanted a equal number of guys to girls.

The Summervilles had a stately home in Passaic, New

Jersey. Margaret was a progressive kind of spirit and got expelled from the Linden School For Girls for smoking. She ended up graduating from Central High much to the displeasure of her parents.

Bud, Tom, Chad and Ellis arrived in Chad's beat up old Ford Model T. Mrs. Summerville was at the door and wasn't impressed by the carnage of a car that had just parked in their driveway. Nevertheless Mrs. Summerville was a gracious host as these boys represented future potential suitors for her daughters.

Margaret came to the door upon hearing that the boys were outside. She was a pretty young woman of seventeen, with a very petite figure. Her cream summer dress with frilly lace looked too childish on her. Bud imagined, from the reputation Margaret had, that her outfit was her mother's choice and not hers. He could only imagine the fight they had to get Margaret to wear it.

Margaret was quick to scoop her cousin and his entourage away from her mother's inquisitive clutches and escort them onto the back lawn where the other girls were waiting.

"Did you bring the demijohn?" She jokingly whispered into her cousin's ear.

Bud nodded while patting the breast pocket of his summer linen suit. His flask was an odd shape of an oval demijohn, and Margaret felt it necessary to tease him as she felt everything else about her cousin was perfect.

The boys were introduced to Ethel, Anna, and Josephine. When Bud introduced Tom, he made sure that everyone knew that the Hardings lived next to Dr. Holm. This seems to give prominence to the sort of character Tom was. However, Bud was keen to omit that Tom's family were Anglican-papalists. It seemed that Chad and Ellis knew Josephine and Anna from previous social functions which left Ethel as the odd girl out.

Tom had previously met Margaret at another social party. He didn't particularly care for Margaret as he felt that she was too forward and flirty. Margaret was unaware of Tom's opinions about her as she had hoped that he would find her engaging enough to be her beau. Margaret made it a point for cousin Bud to include Tom. She felt that she would make such an impression on him that he would ask her out. However, the party didn't go as planned.

Ethel Poole's invite was known as a "filler" in that she was only invited because they needed a fourth and anyone who was anyone was away.

It wasn't that Ethel was plain-looking ; She was just shy. Much to the chagrin of Margaret, Ethel's dress was a little more with the times than Margaret's party dress. It was a teal dress with thin shoulder straps. The dress hung loosely but there was a green sash that tied just below the waist. She wore a pearl necklace but no earrings.

Earlier upon greeting Ethel, Margaret whispered to Anna that Ethel's dress was made with store bought lace to which they both giggled in unison.

What Margaret didn't know was that Ethel had borrowed the pearls from her mother and searched for months in fashion magazines looking for the right dress hoping that someday she would find the perfect occasion to wear it.

Ethel's mother complained that the dress was too elegant for any function she could imagine, her mousey daughter attending, and saw it as a frivolous waste of money. She often commented on how the dress just wasted away in her closet.

Ethel was proud to point out to her mother that the money for the dress wasn't wasted and that the surprise invite to a fancy garden party was the perfect occasion for her to wear it.

Despite the beautiful dress and pearls, Ethel was kept from the girls' inner circle and often stood alone observing the party much the way the boys felt.

Tom took pity on Ethel and chose to escort her to the tent that had the refreshments and food.

Ethel had never been alone at a party before. She was immediately intimidated by Tom's large physique. As they walked towards the tent, she was nervous to be alone with a boy; She wondered what she ought to say. She always feared that her conversations would bore men.

Tom seemed more at ease and initiated the conversation.

When he spoke, he looked straight into Ethel's eyes which made her swoon. He spoke of his graduation ceremony and how boring it was and that he was happy that Adam Goldfarb was made valedictorian.

The way Tom talked allowed her to listen and nod instead of engaging with additional comments. She really liked this way of conversation until the question of her graduation came up. Ethel's heart sank as she had to confess that she was only seventeen and would be graduating next year.

Ethel felt a bit tongue-tied to be in front of one of the most handsome men that she'd ever laid eyes upon. It seemed proper that he should talk, and that she should simply gaze at him.

The tables were set with no name place-settings and the food was buffet style with servers behind each serving area. Although it was an outside sitting, the crystal was from Waterfords of Ireland and the fine china was from Radford of the United Kingdom. Ethel was amazed by the new colorful imitation Imari styled china pattern that was all the rave in modern tableware.

Margaret had turned away from her cousin to see that Ethel was being escorted by Tom.

With a nod of her head to Anna, she made sure that Anna would disrupt Ethel's new acquaintance.

Chad and Anna were the first at the buffet table followed by Tom and Ethel. Anna turned around and spoke with Tom.

"I heard that you are going to attended Columbia," Anna said inquisitively to Tom.

Without waiting for an answer, she added, pulling away from Chad; "I'm going to Barnard."

"Do you think that we should convince Margaret to go to Barnard?" Anna said it loud enough in order in to invite Margaret into the conversation.

"Why whatever should I study?" Margaret said cutting in front of Ethel while helping herself to the Salmon mousse that was on a silver tray in front of them.

Ethel was immediately jealous at the ease of conversation between Tom and the two women and wondered if they would date on campus.

"You should decide on a major first and then find a university that is best suited for it, not the other way around," lectured Tom.

Margaret feeling slighted returned to the safety of her cousin Bud and ignored both Ethel and Tom for the rest of the party.

Ethel's fears seemed to be swept aside as Tom guided her and not Anna through the buffet. He even escorted her to her seat with his hand gently touching her elbow to guide her.

To the timorous Ethel, the party was all a blur with the exception of the clear heavenly vision of Tom, who was constantly at her side.

When everyone played a game of lawn croquet, Tom

was only too eager to guide her with her swing so that she would not embarrass herself for lack of experience with the game.

To Ethel's embarrassment, her parents arrived early to collect her. Had she thought of it, she would have telephoned her father to not come and collect her as she was certain Bud would have given her a ride home. Ethel's mother ingratiated herself into the Summerville's home only to admire the ornate beauty of the stately home.

Mrs. Summerville was quick to assess Mrs Poole as a social climber and declined Mrs. Poole's request for a tour of the house embarrassing Ethel even further. Mrs Poole was too inept to realize that it was very uncouth to ask for a house tour.

When it came time to leave, Tom asked if he may call on her at her home, to which she said yes but then soon panicked realizing that her home was neither stately nor was her family so noble. The Pooles were a middle-class family; Her father owned a haberdashery shop on Broad Street in downtown Newark.

They had a modest house situated between the North and Central wards. Ethel wasn't ashamed of her upbringing or home but rather self-conscious of what Tom might think about their living situation compared to his.

Ethel's Mom chatted away while Ethel sat in the back seat recounting each moment that she had with Tom Harding. Her fantasizing was only disrupted every time her mother asked questions about the party.

"Those girls seemed fast. Don't you agree?"

"I haven't given it any thought," Ethel chimed.

"You know in my day, if you were called a flapper it was an insult to one's character, but today, it's a compliment."

Mrs. Poole laughed to herself over her own comment.

Ethel soon became annoyed as the questions continued: What was served? How many servants did the Summerville's have? And should she write a note to Mrs. Summerville inviting her to lunch?

Ethel was purposely vague with her answers which didn't bother Mrs. Poole as she was happy to hear of any tidbits of news for it was a party she could only dream about as Mrs. Poole grew up poor and such parties were only in her dreams.

With the party over, Ethel retired to her room feeling more sad and alone than usual. It is often ironic that upon meeting someone special, it amplifies how lonely one really is.

Mrs. Poole knocked on Ethel's door but didn't wait for an invite before she entered. She asked for her pearl necklace back to which Ethel unclasped it without any help and returned them to her.

"What's wrong child, you seem so out of sorts?"

Ethel lied to her mother and said that she wasn't feeling well as to tell the truth about Tom would only invite an insurmountable barrage of questioning that Ethel didn't want to confront.

CHAPTER SIX- THE ENCOUNTER

The exterior of the two-story u-shaped apartment building on a street in the Third Ward district housed the backbone of Newark's tough working class society. The complex was named Hensley Court but the sign had long faded above the entrance way. It was situated on a road off of High Street. The section was the poor south side and full of Negroes, Jews, and an assortment of Eastern European immigrants. It was poor but a lively environment and the antithesis of America's melting pot.

Clive had walked into his small but quaint apartment on the second floor bruised, tired and drunk. Dottie, his girlfriend, was sitting on a plush worn-out chair going through a box of chocolates. She was spitting out the ones she didn't like into her hand and placed the already chewed contents back into the box. Next to her the viola was playing some negro upbeat song that was popular at the time. She only looked up when the record skipped.

Her make-up was heavy and her outfit was skimpy. She didn't hear Clive enter.

"Ah, you startled me," she said looking annoyingly at him without getting up.

"Here…"

Clive had a package in his hand which he tossed towards her without warning, causing her box of chocolates to fall to the ground.

"Make dinner."

Clive took off his jacket and tossed it on a rack behind him by the entranceway and pulled a packet of cigarettes from his shirt pocket.

Dottie sucked her teeth in annoyance and went to pick up the fallen chocolates. She then went into the kitchen with the parcel and the chocolates, leaving the music to skip.

Clive lit his cigarette and slumped into the chair that Dottie just exited and skidded the needle off the album.

"Hey!" Dottie cried from the other room.

She returned with a beer and handed it to Clive.

"So, did you win?"

"I did."

Dottie stood right next to him and held out her hand.

"So, where's the money?"

Clive took a tall drink of his beer and lounged into the chair.

"You'll see it later now go make dinner."

Dottie sucked her teeth again and returned to the kitchen.

"You won't believe who was at the Lyric Theatre Boxing Club tonight," He shouted to Dottie.

Dottie didn't answer but he could hear the pots clattering and fridge opening. Clive continued to talk about some young fairy who drove a brand-new shiny green Packard Town car. He went on to explain that he came with another boy who won the amateur event. Clive had never seen them before.

Clive remembered the vision of the effeminate boy. He was like a girl in his mind which confused him, but he couldn't get the boy out of his head. He wondered which mansion in the Forest Hill District did those boys come from. He wondered how rich they were. He fantasized about being rich. He thought of getting rid of Dottie and getting a real classy slender gal to his liking. He wondered if he'd ever see those boys again.

Clive took another swig of his beer and finished it in one gulp and a drag of his cigarette.

"Dottie!"

And almost instinctively she reappeared with another beer. When he pointed to the viola, she knew to put on an album to his liking and then she returned to the kitchen.

Clive heard the sounds of the meat frying in the kitchen. He was hungry and tired and would probably pass out before he could eat the meal.

Dottie returned with a plate of just the cooked steak with some cutlery and a cloth napkin. Clive ate his meal in silence and then went to bed.

In the morning, Dottie was still sleeping when Clive left to go do his regular roofing job. The heat and smell of tarring roofs would have been overwhelming to any man but not to Clive. He was used to it; use to hard labor, heavy smells, and low pay. The smell and the grit blackened everything. Clive's clothes were so dirty that you could barely see the Capital Roofing company name. The company delivered newly cleaned uniforms at the beginning of each week but by the end of the week they blackened beyond recognition. Working above Broad Street, Clive noticed the people exiting the little shops and markets below. He panned the area until his eyes fell upon the same green Packard Town Car that he remembered from the fight. It was in front of Goerke's Department Store.

However, there was a well-dressed chauffeur. He waited until he saw a lady exit from a store followed by a man holding boxes. The chauffeur instinctively got out of the car and opened the door for the middle-aged lady and place the boxes in the front passenger seat.

Clive waited until his lunch break to walk over to the store where he saw the store clerk through the windowed door. Not wanting to enter with his filthy clothes, he motioned to the clerk to come outside.

At first the clerk wasn't sure that the worker was aware this was a refined store but went over to oblige.

"May I help you sir?"

Clive pulled out a cigarette and offered one to the clerk who declined.

"The dame in that Packard with all 'dem boxes, who is she?"

"She is the sister-in-law to Dr. Holm."

Clive thanked him and walked off still smoking his cigarette.

Clive was taking a gamble as he asked around about schools for rich kids and was told of Newark Academy on Market Street.

It was the janitor who told him that most kids went to Sedrick's Diner after school. So Clive took a chance. Upon entry to the diner, he took a booth closest to the window for look-out then he ordered a coffee.

Clive recognized Baxter's face the moment the boy entered. It was burned into his memory.

Up until this point, he didn't know what he was going to say but sometimes things just work themselves out. Baxter almost immediately recognized Clive from billboards and from the only real fight he ever attended.

Clive invited Baxter to join him at a booth. Baxter was hesitant but curious. In order to keep the conversation going, Clive knew to ask about Tom from the boxing match, not knowing it caused a painful pang in Baxter's heart.

Baxter went on to say that Tom and he are high school buddies and he was his sparring partner.

Clive saw that as an invite to offer to spar with Baxter. The look of shock on Baxter's eye's made him realize that that was the wrong thing to say. Baxter clarified what he meant by sparing.

"He really was training me as I have never boxed before."

Clive asked about Baxter's progress in fighting, to which Baxter confessed that he was no longer getting lessons. Clive thought for a while to see how to get an opportunity for him to be with Baxter and one immediately came to mind.

Clive reached into his breast pocket and pulled out a pack of cigarettes. Baxter declined and Clive lit one for himself.

"You're a classy guy, and let's say I need lessons on being like you."

Baxter was confused by what Clive was saying.

"I need to learn to be more fancy, ya' know?"

Baxter looked over the brut of a guy in front of him. Baxter had never spoken in depth with someone so street wise. It was attractive but scary as Baxter imagined that Clive could snap him in two pieces at any moment.

Clive interpreted the hesitancy as not interested.

"Suppose I offer boxing lessons for payment?"

Baxter said that this wouldn't be necessary but confessed that he wasn't sure what he could do for Clive to make him presentable in any of his parent's circles.

Baxter asked for some time to think about it and perhaps meet again. Clive suggested a dinner meeting so that Baxter could teach him table manners. Baxter laughed at the thought but immediately stopped after realizing that Clive was serious.

"Sure."

Just then the waitress arrived with a menu for Baxter.

"I got your meal kid, order anything you want."

Baxter was startled by this offer. Baxter declined his offer and confessed that he only comes for the milkshakes to which Baxter turned to the waitress and ordered two chocolate milkshakes.

The previous night Clive lost heavily at a street craps game. So, he was relieved by not having to pay as he wasn't sure he could cover a meal.

Clive watched the waitress's ass as she walked away but then turned to Baxter.

"When?"

"Excuse me?" Baxter said not understanding.

When can we meet and where?

Baxter had secretly hoped that Clive would have dropped this as he wasn't truly enthusiastic about teaching him anything. Guilt got the best of him and he felt that he should oblige.

"How about Wednesday evening, we can meet for dinner at the Carving Board Restaurant downtown."

"I can't afford that," Clive blurted out.

"Don't worry, I'll treat."

"Geez, thanks kid."

Tom had promised himself that he wouldn't call on Ethel until he was ready. What he meant by ready was to come to Ethel with a free and clear conscious. It was weeks of confessions to reveal deeper thoughts about Baxter and events of the night that lead to their shame. He wanted so badly to try and blame Baxter, but he knew that it wasn't only he who wanted it. So, he knew he couldn't blame his friend.

Eventually, Tom gave up on his conscious and went to see Ethel.

Ethel had given up on waiting for Tom to call on her.

Ethel had faked a headache in order to avoid their arduously mundane task of sitting in the parlour with her parents after supper doing nothing. It was a Sunday spring late afternoon and Ethel was about to write a letter to her grandparents when her mother knocked on her door.

"Ethel, are you feeling better?"

"I'm alright mother, I'm just writing a letter to Grandma Ferris."

Mrs. Poole entered her daughter's neatly organized room. Mrs. Poole was a rather rotund woman with grey hair which she kept in short tight curls. She sat at the edge of the bed.

"You have a gentleman by the name of Thomas Harding to see you. "

With those words Ethel's heart jumped. She ran to the mirror to check her hair and makeup. Knowing that her daughter has never gotten a male visitor before she was eager to assist.

"Do you think he'd like Monclairs dear? I have some chicken salad in the icebox. Do you think he'd like chicken salad sandwich or would he want something sweet?"

Ethel had to think quickly as she didn't want Tom to be kept waiting. So she instructed her mother to serve both as she walked out of the room. Mrs. Poole followed.

Tom was sitting in the front parlour with her father. They both rose when the women entered. Tom was wearing a stripped blazer, white pants and had a boater hat in his hand.

Ethel didn't know whether it was rather plebeian of them not to take his hat. Ethel offered but Tom declined. Tom then gave Ethel a tin box of hard fruit candies from Belle Mead Sweets, a local New Jersey confectionary.

They all sat down with the exception of Mrs. Poole, who excused herself to get some refreshments. Tom and Ethel sat on the sofa while her father sat on the armchair. Ethel was thankful for the gift and promptly opened it to offer to her guest. Tom declined to take one as it was considered in poor taste to take from a gift after it's been presented, but her father eagerly accepted a few pieces of candy when offered.

Tom apologized about the delay in calling but he thought he would have run into her at Long Shore during the summer season. Ethel felt bad having to confess in front of her father that they did not have a summer home but added that they sometimes stay in a hotel out there. Tom said that he had to come back to Newark for some essentials to bring back out to the summer house and thought he'd pay a call.

Mrs. Poole entered with a tray of four beautifully made Monclairs before disappearing back into the kitchen. Mr. Poole divided out the coasters while each person took a glass.

Mrs. Poole then returned with miniature chicken salad sandwiches on plates with doilies and a whole potato pie. Mrs. Poole was going to serve the pie for supper but wanted to impress Ethel's guest.

"What church does your family attend?" asked Mr. Poole.

It was an innocent enough question but it made Tom's heart sink. Tom answered that their family attends Grace Church downtown. Mr. Poole shared that the Poole's attend the Second Presbyterian Church. He was careful to point out that it was located on Washington Street so not to be confused with the First Presbyterian Church.

It seemed that Mr. Poole wanted to engage Tom in conversation, but it was not what Tom wanted to do. However, he obliged the senior and told him about his aspirations for studying medicine at Columbia University.

By then Mrs. Poole had returned and sat on the armchair adjacent to her husband. Tom complimented Mrs. Poole on the food. The conversation was polite and positive.

When Tom got up to leave, Mr. Poole offered Tom a tour of his store and a discount on any hat he would like. Tom thanked Mr. Poole for the offer.

Ethel was glad that her parents let her escort Tom alone to his car.

She wanted to touch him or make some sort of appreciative gesture, but she didn't know what to do.

Tom told her about a summer party happening at Long Shore and wondered if there was anyone Ethel could call upon to stay with if they attended. Ethel asked if she might call him with an answer as she wasn't aware of anyone just yet.

The Carving Board restaurant was located in the Bamberger's Department store which was located on Halsey and Banks street.

It was a trendy place known for their finer cuts of meat. Baxter had gone there once with his mother when he was younger. Although she had enjoyed the meal, she seemed dismissive of the restaurant because they used Maddock's Fine China from Trenton, New Jersey instead of finer china from the United Kingdom.

However, despite his mother's dislike of their fine china selection, she would often have lunch there whenever she was shopping downtown.

Clive was slightly excited about his meeting with Baxter and really curious at what he would order from the menu. Clive was also a great steak-lover and couldn't remember the last time he had a free meal as fancy as this.

Clive arrived early and waited nervously pacing back and forth under the Bamberger's Department store clock. His suit, though well fitting, was rather warn

and slightly frayed. These things were fairly unnotice-
able unless one looked.

The maître'd knew through the reservation the great
Holm family name and where Baxter's party was to sit.
The servers were all male. However, Clive didn't know
that the maître d only escorted, but didn't serve, as he
asked him for more bread while he held Baxter's chair
out for him to sit.

Baxter was slightly embarrassed by this overt display
of attention but didn't mention anything. What he did
mention upon greeting Clive was to instruct him not to
tuck his napkin into his collar.

"Why not? I don't want to get my shirt dirty." Clive
protested.

It's because you should be civil enough not to drop
anything on your shirt.

Clive realized that this was going to be more work than
he anticipated. The waiter arrived with the menu and
Clive was immediately overwhelmed because most of
the words on the menu were in French.

Clive decided to make small talk.

"How did you get the name Baxter?"

Baxter went on to tell the story of how the name is actually the family name of his father's best friend named George W. Baxter, who was once the Governor of Wyoming. They were roommates at the US Military Academy at West Point before Dr. Holm transferred to Yale University.

Another revelation about the menu was that there was wine still being offered despite the prohibition. Clive asked how it was possible to which Baxter replied that restaurants were allowed to deplete their existing stock from prior to 1920. Some of the larger restaurants had huge inventories or bought large inventories prior to the passage of the eighteenth amendment.

Baxter carefully explained the place setting and which forks and spoons were used for what, and the different glassware used for the various beverages.

Clive was more enthralled that he expected. Baxter was mesmerizing as he was elegant and graceful but more importantly very attractive. Clive had never had an opportunity to look at a male like this.

Clive almost had an instinct to protect Baxter but remembered his goal for this encounter. However, Clive was genuinely curious about Baxter as he'd never met his kind in such a setting.

"I know that you like meat so might I suggest the Filet Mignon Messena avec petite pois étuvée?"

"Well I understood the Filet Mignon part but that's about it," scoffed Clive in a joking manner.

Just then the waiter arrived to which Baxter ordered for the both of them. Clive had reluctantly agreed to the Filet Mignon while Baxter ordered the Breast of Chicken Valancay. He also ordered a bottle of Cabernet Sauvignon from the Château Renault

Clive asked if he spoke French and if he knew any other languages.

Baxter replied that he was fluent in French and could read Latin. He went on to explain that Latin was a dead language but was useful in other applications such as medicine and science.

As the meal was a set menu, the appetizers arrived, to which Baxter took the lead and Clive followed attentively.

Clive was thoroughly enjoying what he was learning and thought to replicate it in the future when he had money and could take Dottie out on the town.

Surprisingly, they both enjoyed each other's company and kept the bottles of wine coming non-stop throughout the meal.

By the time the bill came the restaurant was closing and they had gone through four bottles of wine and were quite drunk.

They exited arm and arm from the restaurant. It was raining but neither of them cared. As they walked down the street, they felt their bodies ignited by a strong physical desire. It was late and the city streets were abandoned for a Wednesday night.

Baxter was expecting to be escorted to his car, but Clive had other intensions. Seeing a dark alleyway Clive pulled Baxter into the darkness and started to kiss him passionately. Baxter found the invitation for pleasure a welcome relief as he ran his hands over Clive's muscular body. Clive guided Baxter's hand over his trousers, which was hiding his penis as it was becoming more erect through touch.

Clive pushed Baxter to his knees onto the wet ground and undid his belt and pants button. Baxter unzipped Clive trousers and pulled them down along with his shorts. What surprised Baxter was that Clive's penis was not circumcised. He had never seen an uncircumcised penis before. The head was glistening with moisture and there was a strong pungent order which Baxter didn't like. However, he proceeded to place Clive's penis into his mouth.

Clive let out a pleasurable groan at the feel of Baxter's soft moist mouth. Clive was now yearning for this as if the flood gates of desire were unleashed. The desire from Clive to make this happen was unmeasurable and he began forcefully thrusting his cock into Baxter's mouth until Baxter began choking.

He then pulled Baxter up and undid his pants and shorts and forced him face forward onto the brick wall. The impact of the wall to Baxter's face caused a gash just above his eyebrow but he was too drunk to notice.

Clive ran his fingers along the crack of Baxter's ass until he found the opening he needed. He spit on his finger and jammed it into Baxter anus. This caused an immense shock of pain in Baxter, who let out a yelp only to have his mouth covered entirely by Clive's massive strong hands. Clive gripped Baxter's mouth so tight that later there were bruise marks around his face.

Clive spit on his cock and tried to penetrate Baxter but it was too big to fit and Baxter was clenching too hard.

Baxter thought that he was going to pass out from the pain.

After several attempts by Clive to penetrate Baxter, he began to lose his erection. Soon, he came to his senses about what he was doing and felt he had to get away.

He pushed Baxter to the ground, pulled up his pants and left.

Baxter had passed out.

Several hours later Baxter became conscious of a dog licking his head wound. He got up and was soaking wet. He stumbled to his car and drove home, entering the house through the basement in order not to be seen.

Dr. Holm didn't exactly recognize the name of his new patient but recognized the face the moment Clive entered his office. Dr, Holm read about the prize boxer in the Newark Sunday Call newspaper. Dr. Holm was sitting behind his desk but got up to shake Clive's hand but then sat down and scribbled on his pad. Clive didn't sit which Dr. Holm found odd.

"What can I do for you Mr. Wills?"

"I think it's more of a matter of what can I do for you? "

"I don't understand."

"I want to tell you about your son."

With those words, Dr. Holm put down his pen.

"I seemed to have had an unusual encounter with him. I thought I should bring it to your attention."

Clive went on to talk about the dinner, the drinking, and that Baxter came on to him.

"I'm not going to go to the police. But I want something in return."

Dr. Holm gave Mr. Wills the once over before speaking. His delay made Clive nervous.

"Mr. Wills, what day did this event occur?"

Clive thought that it was a trap but obliged him.

"June 28th," he said with certainty.

"Do you have proof of this transgression?"

Clive said he had a number of witnesses and perhaps more.

"More?"

"Yes, a photo," Clive lied.

"So, you were trying to frame my son?"

Clive became aggressive at the accusation.

"I want money. One hundred in exchange for my silence."

Clive knew that it was a stretch. One hundred was a lot of money, but he was sure Dr. Holm could easily manage it.

Dr. Holm gave Clive another hard stare. He seemed to be considering what he had just said, but Clive knew what the doctor was going to say before he even said it.

"And what if I said that amount was too high? What if I said, 'go ahead and call the police'? It's within your right."

Clive knew that he would refuse the offer, and that was why he had created a backup plan. A different offer. Hit them with an offer that the doctor would refuse, and one that he'll accept. This technique had always worked for him during bribe offer negotiations with bookies on fights. He'd come to rely on it, in a way.

"Come on. You and I both know that the newspapers will care, and this will likely tarnish the fine Holm family name.

"Alright, I'll accept your offer under the condition that you meet me at my house tonight at seven this evening. I want my son present. If this is in fact true, he'll confess. My son has never lied to me."

Clive nodded and reached out his hand to which Dr. Holm declined to take. Clive left and Dr. Holm sat down deep in thought.

Baxter was unaware of what had transpired earlier but he sensed something different about his father over dinner.

"We're going to have a guest at seven tonight. I would like you to be present," Dr. Holm said coldly.

"Who is it?"

"I cannot say."

After dinner, Baxter went to his room and waited. At 6:55 pm he looked out his window and panicked. Clive was walking up the walkway. The doorbell rang but Baxter remained in his room until his father called him down.

Dr. Holm was waiting for his son in the front parlour doorway Baxter expected that he would have met Clive in his office. As Baxter entered, he saw Clive sitting on the sofa closest to the front window. He stood up when Baxter entered but didn't make eye contact. It would seem that he was ashamed of being there.

Dr. Holm closed the sliding doors to the parlour and didn't order drinks. In fact, he told the staff that they were to remain downstairs until called upon.

"I believe you know Mr. Wills."

Baxter just sat on the chair furthest from Clive. They didn't shake hands. Baxter nodded in the affirmative.

"This morning, Mr. Wills came to my office saying that you made sexual advances towards him. Mr. Wills also said that he would have gone to the police …"

Baxter was so stunned by these statement that he forgot to defend his honour by adding that it was Clive who initiated the advance not he.

"The police?" Baxter said in a shocked manner.

"… but insisted that he would remain silent on the incident. He said the transgression occurred on June 28th, is this correct?"

Baxter was silent. This was the first time that Baxter took a hard look at his father. It wasn't that Dr. Holm didn't try to be a good father. He wanted to be a good father but just didn't know how to connect with Baxter.

In public, his father was stoic in nature whereas Baxter was warm kind and easily showed emotion. Dr. Holm questioned why Baxter had these mannerisms. He believed it would not help a man in such a tough world.

He felt that he was the wrong son for Dr. Holm and felt this every time they interacted. But the truth was that he loved his father but he didn't necessarily like him. This is a truth in life many share but rarely come to such a conclusion at such a young age.

The pain of this incident was that it reinforced all the negative stereotypes that his father saw in him. This bothered him more than being caught in the sexual act himself.

Baxter cleared his throat. A rage came over him internally, but he kept his composure.

"Father, we drank too much and I'm not certain that it was I who initiated the misdeed."

Upon hearing his words, Clive jumped to his feet and ran towards Baxter.

"That's a lie!" Clive shouted.

However, he was intercepted by Dr. Holm.

"If you want your money, you will sit down and be civil."

"I need a drink!"

"I hope you will excuse my discourtesy but in the manner that you are in my house, I will decline to offer you one Mr. Wills."

Clive sat down again, pulling out a handkerchief to wipe the sweat off the brow of his face.

At this point, Baxter could only question his own naive judgement in trusting Clive. The irony was that Baxter now saw Clive as the one being weak-willed for declaring such an audacious perversion of what had transpired.

Baxter felt sorry for Clive but was unrepentant in his own version. Baxter saw through his facade as Clive spoke more and more as if it was confession of guilt and not one of moral justice.

Dr. Holm walked to a serving table where there was a piece of paper waiting.

"Mr. Wills, I have taken the liberty of drawing up a document to which you must read. It basically assures me that in exchange for $100 you will keep your silence on the event of June 28th and make no further mention or accusations about it. Please look it over and sign at the bottom. If you agree to it, sign your full name and address."

Baxter objected but Dr. Holm continued.

Clive walked over to where Dr. Holm had the document with a fountain pen beside it.

Clive quickly looked it over and Dr. Holm presented five crisp twenty dollar bills for him.

Clive greedily took the money and stuffed it in his pocket after signing the paper.

"Now get out and I wish never to see you again."

Clive looked at Baxter and for some reason said, "Sorry." However, Baxter just looked away.

Dr. Holm opened the parlour door and escorted Clive out the front door. He then returned to the parlour.

"I wanted you to see that so that we have an understanding."

Baxter, for the first time, saw that his father relished in his hatred of him. He knew that no matter what he will ever do, whatever success, he made of his life, his father would always hate him.

Dr. Clive went on in a monotone manner as if he had recited what he was saying. He instructed Baxter to do the right thing and find a proper woman to marry. And, if he did not find a suitable woman by the end of summer, he would be cut off from his allowance and his inheritance. He would, furthermore, be banished from the house.

"Have I made myself clear?"

Baxter bowed his head and said "Yes."

CHAPTER SEVEN- THE FAVOUR

The last time Tom saw Baxter, it was during graduation ceremonies at Newark Academy. The families said their pleasantries to each other but nothing further. They went onto separate celebratory functions.

So, it was a shock for Tom to see Baxter from his bedroom window walking towards his house. Baxter stopped to greet his kid brother William, who was playing in the yard.

Tom immediately ran downstairs to meet him.

"I need to talk to you." Baxter said.

"About what?"

"I need to ask you a favour. I need to find a girlfriend." Baxter pleaded.

The request took Tom completely by surprise. Tom felt a tinge of emotion that he hadn't felt before towards Baxter but was scared to acknowledge what it was. Instead, he felt that this was an offer from Baxter to put whatever happened between them in the past and to move forward.

"I'm glad that you came to me. I think that would be best for you, too."

"I know that Ethel and I are going to the Essex's Club for their July fourth Banquet over at Hutton Park. We are guests of the Kemps, perhaps I can get you an invite?"

Baxter was equally surprised by Tom's disclosure of a girlfriend. He had mixed emotions and a sort of curiosity about any girl in which Tom would be interested.

"I would much appreciate that. Ethel? I don't know her."

Tom went on to explain how he met Ethel at Bud's cousin Margaret's garden party in Passaic. As he explained it, he felt a strange feeling come over him as he was explaining how he met her. He went on to say that Ethel doesn't know anyone there, but Margaret would definitely know of some girls suitable for him.

Baxter looked away but expressed his appreciation to Tom. The expression almost sounded like a deep sigh instead of an enthusiastic reply.

On the morning of Independence Day, It was decided that they would take the Holm's Packard Town car but without the chauffeur as it was the largest and most luxurious car. Bud and Josephine were to ride along too. Bud Cronheim was now officially dating Josephine Woodlow.

Ethel didn't have a suitable dress to wear and worried what the other girls would think of her plain outfit. Ethel was told that Tom would come around eleven in the morning to fetch her. Ethel was ready by ten and waited with her parents in their living room. As eleven approached, Mr. Poole went to the window with each sound of a car passing.

"Oh sit Earl, you're making us nervous." Mrs. Poole pestered while knitting nervously in her chair.

By eleven fifteen, Ethel grew worrisome and irritable. When her mother suggested that she call over to the Hardings, she snapped at her mother for suggesting it and ran upstairs crying.

Ethel felt that her chance at love was over before it began. Her mother quickly came to console her. As she assured her daughter that everything would be alright, a large automobile pulled into the driveway.

Ethel quickly dried her eyes and checked herself in the mirror before departing downstairs with her mother. The Pooles followed their daughter to the car but for different reasons. Mr Poole wanted to admire the fine automobile, whereas Mrs. Poole wanted to ingraciate herself with the young entourage.

It was Mrs. Poole's forward suggestion that embarrassed Ethel the most. Not only did she invite everyone in the car to a summer party at the Poole residence, but she made sure all of them immediately committed to coming.

Ethel was relieved when the car began to back out of the driveway as the Poole's followed the car's slow retreat from their home waving to them as they left.

While driving to the Essex Country Club Josephine complained about having to go, and worried that there would be too many mosquitos as the country club was near the shore. Bud retorted that there was a large lake there, but this seemed only to embolden Josephine's fear of mosquitos.

Ethel silently worried about her outfit as she didn't really have "country club" attire. She borrowed a dress from her mother but felt is seemed a bit dated.

The shin length dress was made from a creamed coloured fabric set in contorted shape. The style seemed to mimic the fashion from the previous decade because it still had an emphasis on the bust which modern styles avoided.

Her mother insisted that it was the proper outfit for a 4th of July event but her mother has never been to a country club before.

They arrived around 2:00 pm and were immediately segregated in to groups of boys and girls. The Essex Country Club was the premier club in all of New Jersey. Its members included the New Jersey Governor, judges, and several state representatives. But with all the wealth, none of them could buy good weather. It became cloudy and windy which bode well for Josephine as she knew mosquitos hated the wind.

Chad Kemp was already there waiting since his family was hosting the party. He flashed the inside of his coat to the approaching group to reveal the silver flask hidden away, to which Tom and Bud flashed theirs. The girls were to set up some game, which the boys were not privy to see. Chad suggested that the boys go down to the lake and take out the row boats. Tom protested as they were all in white linen pants, but Chad had one of the servers bring them blankets to protect their pants.

It was a short hike to the lake and the row boats were. Chad and Bud got into one boat and Tom and Baxter got into another. There were already some boats out on the water. Chad recognized his uncle in one of them and rowed feverishly to reach them leaving Tom and Baxter behind.

Once in the boat, Tom and Baxter realized that this was awkward as they have been avoiding each other all summer.

But to Tom it meant something different because before him was the man who changed everything about him. Baxter was the man who made him realize how lonely he was and how he questioned everything he stood for.

Tom's heart beat with a certain angst that couldn't be explained. He was looking at the very thing he was trying to run away from. His true feeling. Tom thought to say some hail Mary's in his head but couldn't somehow bring himself to do it.

Tom was rowing while Baxter stared out onto the water. Every now and again, they would catch each looking at the other.

After a long and silent pause that Tom could no longer bear, he asked:

"Do you know the 70 times 7 rule from the Bible?"

"No, what is it?"

Tom went on to explain that in the Book of Matthew, Peter asks Jesus:

"Lord, how many times shall I forgive my brother or sister who have sinned against me?"

And Jesus replied

"I say not unto thee, until seven times: but, until seventy times seven."

Baxter was confused by this statement.

"What does that mean?" Baxter asked.

"That God said we are only allowed to be forgiven for up to 490 sins in our lifetime."

Have you counted your sins? Tom asked.

Baxter didn't answer.

Tom goes on to say that it would be best to stay with the sins that you have and to not go any further.

"I've never asked this and I hope that you won't take offence but are you a man of God?" Tom asked breaking the long silence.

The question threw Baxter. Until this moment, Tom and Baxter never spoke of religion with the one exception when Tom asked why his father didn't arrange for a wake before his mother's funeral. To which Baxter explained that wakes are for Catholics.

Tom remembered that conversation because it was at that moment Baxter inadvertently instilled a sense of religious inferiority into Tom psyche.

Tom always wished that his family were traditional protestants and hated the stigma that came with being an Anglo-papalist. He felt that his religious upbringing in a way excluded his family from the inner circles of high society.

"I don't know what you mean by 'man of God' but I go to church. I do my prayers and my family tithe." Baxter replied.

"Yes, but is there a passion for God in you?"

"By the way you are saying this, you act as if there is something lacking in me."

"I'm sorry that wasn't my intent."

Tom wasn't exactly sure where he was trying to steer the conversation. So, he tried a different approach.

"When I was younger, I wanted to be a Catholic priest," Tom confessed.

It was at that moment of nervousness from Tom that one of the oars slipped out of the rigger causing a splash of water to cascade beside them.

Baxter was surprised by this random confession.

"Why?"

"Because you only have one commitment and that would be to God."

Baxter was not really understanding the gist of the conversation and wondered if this was stemming from their sexual encounter. Yet, he didn't dare break the silence between them about that night.

"Tom, I feel that you are trying to get an answer from me but you don't know how to pose the question."

At that moment, Tom realized how intelligent and more emotionally mature Baxter was compared to himself.

"I guess I wondered if you would ever consider following a more religious path with me."

Tom's heart beat frantically waiting for an answer. In Tom's mind, this was the only solution to what's eating at his soul. Tom wanted a closeness with Baxter that would be accepted by both society and God.

Baxter now understood what Tom was thinking. He concluded that Tom was correct that his spiritual path was more reverent than his own. He also saw the vulnerability Tom was displaying right now and that their drunk encounter had had just as deep an impact on Tom as it did with him.

Baxter worded his answer carefully.

"Tom, I don't think that I would enter into an ecclesiastical order to escape the reality of our true selves."

Tom knew that Baxter was absolutely correct in his assessment. Tom was silently ashamed at himself for asking. They continued to row in silence.

When they returned, a literal maze was set up where each couple had to go through and answer clues at each stop to progress further. Baxter was paired with a girl named Clara de Villepin. Although Clara spoke perfect French and English without an accent on either side, he was paired with her only because he was the only one of Bud's friends who spoke fluent French. She was yet another cousin of Bud's. Where one could see the similarities between Bud and his cousin Margaret, Clara had absolutely no similar features to Bud. Bud and Margaret had dirty blond hair with pale skin. Bud also had freckles. Yet Clara had beautiful skin, tanned to a golden hue by the sun. Her hair was jet black and bobbed in the latest style. When the wind blew her hair, it seemed to always go perfectly back into place like in the movies. She was exquisitely dressed. Where as the other girls wore white summer dresses. Clara wore a drop waist tea green pastel coloured dress. The hem length was just below the knee.

Clara's family lived in Greenwich, Connecticut.

When presented to Baxter, she was rather sure of herself. Baxter wasn't used to such women. She was far advanced for her years. Many of the bachelors who arrived stag paid her courtesies, but she ignored them and stuck close to her assigned partner, Baxter, which in turn made him seem popular among the crowd.

As the game started, Clara wasn't bashful about knowing the answers. She didn't wait for Baxter to make the first suggestions either. They were quite a team and they paced ahead of everyone to win the game.

Baxter seemed at ease with Clara but had no intention of thinking that she was truly available. His thoughts were about what he ought to do to show interest in her but never felt he had the opportunity.

When the night was over, he offered to call on her and she politely accepted.

CHAPTER EIGHT - THE BISEXUAL

With the hundred dollars, Clive had thought that Dottie would have been delighted but instead their relationship crumbled under her new list of demands. They both started drinking more but for different reasons.

For Clive, he drank to wipe away the disgust and regret for the actions he had done. He knew that Baxter only had the best of intentions for him, and Clive saw a weakness and went for it.

For Dottie, she drank because she was suffocating in their relationship. She felt that Clive's handling of the situation exposed how ignorant he was and that he had sold them short. When presented with the five crisp bills, she asked if they would be getting $100 monthly payments. When Clive said that it was a one-time exchange, she screamed at him in anger.

The money only amplified the drift that already existed between them. Clive knew that he was getting older and that his best fighting years were behind him. He was sick of slugging hot, smelly, skin staining, tar but didn't want to work for the underground world of the gangsters either.

He saw his options as being few and far between, but the visit to the Holm's estate showed him what could have been. He wondered if he could have gone through with being Baxter's companion.

Although the incident was set up in his mind from the get go, the outcome left him a different man. He felt Baxter was a good kid and didn't deserve what he had done to him.

Clive spent more time than he cared to admit thinking over the incident and he wondered what would have happened if it had been better planned.

He remembered Baxter's softness and smell. These after thoughts sexually aroused him which he found as a rather strange and foreign sensation.

Clive's solution to handling Dottie was to supply her with booze and lots of it. He was able to get cases of it from his bookie connections for cheap prices in appreciation for fixed matches.

But, as time progressed, she got worse, almost intolerable. Clive found himself not wanting to go home after a night out.

One night, Clive stumbled into the speakeasy around 1am. It was surprisingly quiet but it was a weeknight.

He took a table in the back for solitude, but he wasn't alone for long.

She might have been beautiful once before the years of hard life gave her crow's feet and sagging cheeks. She had entered the bar eyeing the joint until she laid eyes on Clive.

She whisked by the bartender without even ordering but the bartender knew her type. He called her kind by the vulgar term of "moocher coochies"

"Hey, aren't you that famous boxer?"

She knew his kind and knew to stroke his ego early.

"Ya, who's asking?"

"I'm Bunny hun, I've seen you in the ring a few times. You're quite the man up there." She lied.

Bunny only knew him from flyers around town.

Clive gave her the once over as he was drunk and struggling to focus.

Her smile revealed the cracks that extended around her lips, filled in with cheap lipstick giving her an uneasy smile. However, the longer she smiled, the more genuine it looked and he eventually found himself smiling.

His smile was her queue to reel him in. She motioned the bartender for two drinks.

'I guess I'm buying,' Clive said as she settled into the chair sliding it closer to him.

"Honey, I'm worth it; I'm good company," she said with a wink.

Just then the bartender arrived with a bottle of whiskey and two shot glasses.

Clive paid him immediately.

It had been a while since Clive fucked any woman besides Dottie and he couldn't even recall the last time they had sex. Dottie would often give him drunken blowjobs if she wanted something from him. However, he struggled to recall the last time they had full sexual intercourse.

"You know what I miss Honey? I miss a nice bottle of Champagne.

Bunny went on to talk about how she worked at this resort in Upstate New York where they served the finest of foods but the best champagne New York had to offer.

"Now what was the name of that champagne…oh yeah, The Brotherhood that was really nice bubbly!"

'I think we all miss those days' Clive laughed.

Bunny slammed back a shot and poured herself another finishing off the bottle

Clive waved to the barman who had nothing better to do except to watch them drunkingly flirt with one another.

The barman instinctively came with another bottle.

Bunny reached over and felt Clive's legs. Clive offered to pour her another shot.

As Clive poured, he got another good look at Bunny. He knew that her best years were well behind her but was reminded just how much he was no longer youthful. He wasn't the prize fighter he used to be.

As they finished the bottle, Clive thought it was worth planting the seeds he hoped to sow soon.

"So, do you live close to here?"

"Oh, I'm closer than you think,' Bunny said while fiirtively placing her index finger on Clive's lip. No strings on me and the ones you pull gets this dress off'

"Well let me pulls some strings then," said Clive confidently as if all would go well. Clive got up to leave.

Bunny knew to follow. She smiled and looked off into the distance. 'My place ain't much but it's home' She glanced at Clive as if expecting him to sympathize about her situation.

'No need to worry, we can keep the lights out if you want,' he said, hoping it was enough.

Although it was a short walk to her place, the number of stairs they had to climb was rather overwhelming for the two drunks. Upon entering her flat, Clive felt suddenly tired.

Although they agreed to keep the lights off. Bunny instinctively turned on a table lamp.

The room seemed a little warmer in the light with all its dark corners. Her place was a refurbished hotel room, but Clive didn't mind.

"This way, " said Bunny as she escorted a Clive to her bedroom. Once in her room, she was the one who made the first move and he was grateful. She was lonely and he was tired. It was too much work all of the sudden to try and seduce her.

Clive turned away and busied himself undressing and flicking off the light. She wanted to be strategically under the covers as not to show her wrinkles or sagging breasts.

"How about a kiss?" Clive slid under the covers to join her.

She smelled of booze and B.O. He kissed her lightly and proceeded to pushed her head down under the covers towards his flaccid penis.

In the dark, with her down below sucking his penis, Clive's drunken mind drifted. It drifted to the thought of Baxter. Whereas there he failed to perform, it was ironic that the thoughts of this young man made his penis hard.

Bunny thought that her magic mouth was what brought on the erection. She pushed up to kiss him again and then rolled on her back for him to mount her which he did.

Clive had no problem entering Bunny. He thought her vagina a bit to loose but wasn't sure that was attributable to age or use.

After a while, they both passed out. He was still inside her but she, at some point, pushed him off as he was too heavy.

He woke up early and snuck out without even saying good-bye.

While Clive was away, Dottie called John Washington, a known local negro boxing celebrity that she had met during his match against Clive.

John treated different differently. For starters, he was a good listener. Her main want from her relationship with Clive was to be appreciated for all that she does. Dottie knew that her relationship with John would be taboo otherwise she would have left Clive years ago.

Things had reached a breaking point and when Clive accosted her one night, she took a cab straight to John's place to recuperate. At John's place, she was pampered and happy. John knew how to cook, and they often cooked together.

John was always sad to see her go back to Clive. It broke his heart, but he understood his role in society and Dottie was heartbroken because of it.

One thing was certain, when Dottie was with John, she didn't drink as much. Clive's failure to secure a good regular payment from the Holms was the deciding moment for her to leave him.

However, Dottie's one flaw in her plan was that she wanted to have it out one last time. A final goodbye but little did she know how final it would be.

The sober walk home provided the first moment of clarity that Clive has ever had in his entire life. Clive's mother died while giving birth to him. His father was a violent drunk who felt the only thing he could pass onto his son was a thick skin.

And yes, the beatings did toughen him but it also made Clive believe that any softness in men was a vulnerability. This was because if Clive ever cried while getting a beating, his father felt that it was his duty to beat his son even harder.

This gave Clive the warped perspective that weakness in men should be taken advantage of, just as he did with Baxter.

Yet, with Baxter there was something different that he hadn't seen in any other man that he encountered. An oxymoronic softness that was the young boy's strength. It was the first time that Clive saw pure goodness, pure innocence in a man, which was an attribute he gave to no one, not even women.

To Clive, his was a world of exploitation whether it was bootlegging, fixing fights or bribing others. This was Clive's motto for existence but he never questioned whether or not it was a noble or good act until he encountered Baxter.

He realized that with all the training Baxter would have given him and with all the money he could garner, he would never be a man of good character like Baxter.

The very action of Baxter's offer to help make him a better person showed proof that such good men do exist.

He wished that he would have met a guy like Baxter years ago. Would it have made a difference in Clive's view of the world? He didn't have an answer for that as this was the first time that Clive ever felt remorse for his actions.

Clive wanted to be the man who protect Baxter from a ruffian like himself.

But during this long moment of introspection, Clive forgot about the drunken sexual element of thoughts about Baxter that gave him the erection needed to penetrate Bunny.

Yes, Clive felt hurt and regret for his actions. He would have drunk these thoughts away. This was how he was raised to deal with emotions, but being severely hungover the very thought of booze nauseated him.

He felt that he deserved to wallow in these feelings for what he had done to Baxter. And wallow he did as he walked home.

Clive was relieved when he got home early in the morning to find that Dottie wasn't there.

CHAPTER NINE - THE DEATH

Ethel sensed that her relationship with Tom wasn't what she had hoped for. Tom had made a drunk confession over dinner one night to her that he only dated her because he felt sorry for her. He tried to apologize, and blamed booze as the reason why he said it but since then they haven't been the same.

However, long before the drunken confession, Ethel knew that something was amiss between them. Tom was thoughtful, caring, and courteous, but it seemed out of duty instead of sincerity. There seemed to be no innate desire for Tom to be with her. She knew something was wrong which she kept quietly to herself.

In Ethel's mind, the end of summer garden party that she was hosting was supposed to be their engagement party, but a proposal never materialized from Tom.

It was going to be the last party of the summer season as it was already mid-August.

Ethel just relinquished to the joy that she had made friends albeit because she was dating Tom and his social circle but nonetheless, she seemed to feel like she was popular.

The Pooles knew they had one chance to shine and didn't spare any expense. Although they didn't have servants or a large yard, they really dressed up their garden to reflect a fun, cheery atmosphere.

Tom arrived early to help and Ethel really appreciated the effort that he put in. To Mr. and Mrs. Poole, Tom was the perfect potential son-in-law that they wanted: attentive, rich, and the envy of all the other parents who wanted a guy just like Tom for their daughters. Tom even borrowed extra utensils and items from his parents' home.

Although not really a couple, Baxter arrived alone, and Clara arrived with "the girls." But they stuck together during the party.

Bud, Chad, and Ellis did their ceremonial secret re-vealing of their flasks filled with alcohol as they did at every party.

Margaret and Josephine were genuinely pleasant which was a surprise because Bud feared Josephine was going to complain about "slumming it" in Central District Newark.

Although there wasn't much room in their yard, the Pooles set up a croquet set and Tom and the boys in-stinctively went to play that first.

The boys would slip out with each girl to get behind the garage for a quick swig of booze from whosever flask was available for the taking.

Tom's mental freedom from Ethel and the pressures of steering the two of them towards a proposal left time to think about Baxter again. However, with this set up, it seemed a safe distance for him to think without feeling guilty.

From the time that Ethel sent out the invitations, Tom had imagined every scenario for speaking to Baxter. They hadn't seen each other since the July 4th party at the country club.

In one, Baxter saw Tom and approached with the warmest of hugs confessing that he missed him. In another, he ignored Tom entirely. In yet another, Baxter would show up with a new, dashing girlfriend.

When Tom did see him, though, they just shook hands. They exchanged pleasantries.

"So, what's new with you?"

Tom demurred "same old."

"Have you been traveling?" Baxter asked politely.

"A bit. Virginia to see my mom's family."

Tom waited for him to ask more about his life. He wanted more. Instead, he settled into silence.

Tom crossed his arms. They averted each other's gaze from behind their sunglasses.

Clara came over to rescue Baxter, making Tom paranoid that he did something wrong.

Baxter excused himself. Their one requisite conversation at the garden party was over.

The blankness of Baxter's sunglasses stare and the unsettling monotone in his voice made Tom question his sanity. Had he imagined that drunken night of sex in Baxter's car?

Tom wished he had seen some mischievous, jovial glint in Baxter's eye. Some small chuckle. Tom used to have the power to make him laugh.

Now it was as though Tom had never existed for him at all. Those maddening, wildly happy years of growing up together and all through high school carried off in a hearse. It occurred to Tom then that to be erased was worse than to be remembered for that one sinful encounter.

Tom watched Baxter on and off across the party only taking breaks to sneak behind the garage with Ethel or Bud to drink from the one of three almost empty flasks.

Tom was getting drunk and worried the truth would come out. Tom tended to do his best confessions to whomever when drunk.

Then it all changed.

A car arrived and Tom couldn't even remember who it was. He just remembered Mrs. Poole calling out for Baxter.

Something was wrong and Tom knew it. He followed the unknowingly cheerful Baxter into the house where a police officer announced that his father had died from an apparent heart attack.

Tom saw Baxter's face drain. Baxter was numb. Tom suggested that he take his keys and drive Baxter home.

When Baxter didn't answer, Tom shouted: "Keys, keys, give me your keys."

Baxter reached into his pocket and held out the keys.

Tom took over. He took Baxter by the arm and escorted him towards his car.

By now, a crowd had gathered giving their condolences, but Tom knew Baxter didn't hear any of it. He just gave polite monotone thanks to each who spoke to him as they were leaving. Clara was the last to say something and even hugged Baxter but he didn't hug her back.

Tom gently placed Baxter in the passenger seat of Baxter's car and got in the driver's side.

It was a short drive to Baxter's home where the servants were waiting in the entrance way.

Tom was a bit rude but ordered the servants to go downstairs unless called.

The phone rang but Tom shouted to the parlour maid to take a message.

Tom felt it best to take Baxter somewhere familiar which was Baxter's bedroom. It had been years since Tom had been in Baxter's room.

Once the door closed behind them Baxter fell apart.

He collapsed into Tom's arms crying, wailing.

Tom held him tight.

"He didn't love me but now I have nothing." Baxter said in between sobs.

"No, he loved you." Tom said trying to be supportive, but it didn't help. Baxter fell limp and cried from a deep sorrow like a pool of loneliness had been inside him for so long.

Tom knew this feeling. He understood him.

"I'm all alone," Baxter said.

"No, you're not. You have me. You've always had me, but I was afraid to admit it."

"Tom, please don't leave me. Don't ever leave me. God, I need you."

Tom gently rocked him. He then walked to the hall phone to ring to the downstairs servants' quarters. He made sure that the bedroom door was open so that Baxter could still see him and not feel abandoned.

Tom didn't know who picked up but asked who was familiar enough with Dr. Holm's things to know where he kept the sedatives.

Tom then returned to Baxter's bedroom and laid down and held him.

Moments later there was a knock at the door. It was the cook with a glass of water and a powder.

She instructed Tom to stir the powder in to the glass of water until it dissolved completely and for Baxter to drink it all.

Tom thanked her and she disappeared quickly.

Tom followed her instructions and gave Baxter the sedative solution.

However, it probably wasn't needed. The raw emotion had drained Baxter and he quickly fell asleep.

Tom stayed with Baxter the entire night, only to answer the occasional knock from servants when they were leaving or if there were important messages like the hospital was transferring Dr. Holm's body to the coroner's or that so and so would be coming to see Baxter tomorrow.

Tom slept very little that night in Baxter's small twin bed. He feared the guilt from the past would rear its ugly face into his mind but it didn't. He thought about all those confessions, all those prayers were wasted energy.

Tom blamed himself for their separation. He now knew his true feelings for Baxter and a peaceful calm fell over him.

The next day Tom wrote a letter to Ethel. Tom knew it to be crass to end a relationship by letter but he his love and loyalty were with Baxter now. He pushed Baxter to eat, to shower, and to face the world.

There were so many visitors and arrangements to be made. It was overwhelming and when Baxter pulled back because it was too much, Tom stepped in and took over.

At times, they would just stare into each other's eyes.

Tom was carrying Baxter through life now.

Baxter knew this and was appreciative, but he worried when it was going to end.

When there was a private moment with just the two of them, Tom kissed Baxter on the forehead and told him not to worry.

Sometimes Baxter cried uncontrollably, and Tom would hold him and rock him.

Tom's brother brought over changes of clothing for him as he spent several nights at the Holm's residence.

Dr. Holm was laid in state for two whole days. At times, there were lines down the driveway and around the corner.

Tom met people who Dr. Holm delivered, operated on, practiced with, and his childhood friends. There were politicians, clergy, and families from all walks of life.

The funeral was held at Trinity Church. It was standing room only.

Baxter wanted Tom to be present when there was a reading of the will. Baxter was to inherit over $250,000 plus the property from the estate. There was also a separate trust to be paid to Baxter from the death of his mother.

To Baxter it all meant nothing to him. He was focused on how Tom cared for him. It was what he dreamed of all along.

Tom confessed to Baxter that he broke up with Ethel over a week ago.

The next week, when it was safe enough for Baxter to be left alone, Tom left to go make arrangements at Columbia University. He made sure to explain to Baxter that he'd be catching the Hudson Tube but coming back after he was done.

It was the first time Baxter was alone without Tom and he was okay with it. Their time together was heavenly and their love making had progressed into something of a good routine of growth and sexual development.

Baxter knew that Tom was his.

CHAPTER TEN - THE CHOICE

A generation ago there were absolutely strict rules for mourning, and in this respect no one who believed in the propriety of the conventions would have broken them. However, well into the 1920s, every phase of life was being reexamined in the light of individual opinion, so that even mourning had become largely a question of personal feeling and the ultimate decision rested with the individual.

Baxter had used the customs of mourning to his advantage. His aunt Grace, his mother's sister, offered to stay once again with him but Baxter was adamant that she didn't. In fact, they almost had a falling out as she pressed Baxter to accept her invitation to stay with him.

Baxter followed the custom of placing a black wreath on the door and drawing all curtains.

It had been two weeks since the funeral and Tom had moved most of his clothes over to Baxter's home.

It had generated little suspicion since it would be natural for a friend to care for another in mourning. It was also helpful that the Holms didn't keep overnight staff to snoop about.

With the curtains drawn and after the servants had left for the day, Tom and Baxter were free to roam the house at night together and express whatever affection they wanted towards each other.

By day Baxter was going through the various affairs dealing with the estate, placing notices in the various papers announcing the death of his father, closing his father's office, and tending to endless bereavement cards that arrived at his home.

It was on one particular hot summer day that Baxter received a visitor he hadn't expected. He was going through his father's closets with the chambermaid pulling out clothes to donate when the parlour maid came to say that there was a Clive Wills to see him.

It was at that moment that he regretted allowing Tom to leave him. He could have told the maid to say that he wasn't seeing visitors right now but instead went downstairs to see him.

Clive was waiting in the same living room he had been during that first meeting where he witnessed him taking the blackmail money for his silence.

Clive sat up the moment Baxter entered.

It was Clive's eyes that searched into Baxter's soul to see if there was some sort of forgiveness.

He was wearing a striped shirt that hugged his torso tightly revealing his well-defined muscles, suspenders that were holding up white slacks. He took his cap off when he saw Baxter enter.

"I guess I'd be the last person that you'd want to see," said Clive as he came forward to greet him.

Baxter instructed the parlour maid to instruct all the staff to wait downstairs until called upon. He then closed the sliding parlour doors.

Baxter extended his hand to greet him. He then motioned Clive to sit.

"I guess I'm just curious to hear what you have to say."

Clive said that he had read in the paper about his father's death. He knew that he did Baxter wrong but wanted Baxter to know that he was ashamed for it.

He even offered to give the money back.

But then he did something that was totally out of character. He got up and kneeled before Baxter. He pushed himself forward so that he was kneeling between Baxter's legs.

"I'm here for you," Clive said softly while embracing Baxter. Baxter didn't return the affection, nor did he push him away.

Baxter was wise as not to provoke the anger he had seen displayed from this brute of a man when they were last in this parlour.

Clive misinterpreted this lack of gesture on Baxter's part as hesitancy of the heart. So, he took Baxter's hand and guided it to his well-defined chest.

"I understand," said Baxter "but you must give me time."

"So, there is hope for us?"

"I don't know."

"I know that I'm not worthy of you but give me a chance…"

Baxter corrected him "Another chance?"

Those words hurt Clive as no other person did before. It was the invisible punch he was always warned about that came not in the boxing ring but beyond the physical and deep into the soul.

Clive reached into his pocket and gave Baxter a gift. It was a cheaply crafted flask with Baxter's initials on it. However, the spacing was meant for three letters to include the middle initial, making just the two initials seem poorly placed as Clive didn't know Baxter's middle name.

Baxter smiled and thanked him.

"Shall we start my lessons again? I want to learn how to be proper and worthy for you."

Baxter walked him to the door only with a, "Perhaps, you have to give me time," statement.

Dottie waited for the familiar sound of Clive's key opening the front door. She had been waiting for him.

Her bags were packed, and she was sitting in the worn out chair in their living room, drinking.

Now and again she would glance up at the clock, but without anxiety, merely to please herself with the thought that each minute gone by made it nearer the time when she would be free.

She wanted to see the look on his face. Would it be shock? Would it be sorrow?

She revelled in this thought as she took another swig of her drink.

The apartment had been cleaned, tidied, and put into order. It was the cleaning the apartment needed in years but she knew Clive wouldn't even appreciate that.

When the sound of keys finally did come into play, Dottie was too drunk to react.

Clive was standing before her, before she could even get her words out.

"This is where I say goodbye," she slurred.

Clive looked at the packed bags that were right beside her.

"This comes as no surprise since you drained the bank account of our rent money."

Dottic laughed.

"I've earned that money putting up with you for all these years. Your beatings, your neglect your stupidity."

Clive felt his blood boil and his fist clenched, but he kept his composure.

"And where are you going?" He asked.

"Ha" Dottie blurted out.

The heavy alcohol smell on her breath made Clive realize she wouldn't get far.

Dottie then confessed to him about John Washington. The man that she felt deserved her.

She even listed what he has done for her sexually and where Clive was lacking.

"All this while you were with me, seeing him, which makes you a whore."

Dottie's eyes flashed as she leaped forward and slapped Clive across the face with all the strength she could muster.

However, his powerful physique weathered the blow easy. Clive didn't flinch once.

Dottie then raised her arm a second time, but as her hand came swinging towards him, he blocked it and was even able to push her back against the mantel piece. She recovered quickly and came flying at him again.

In a moment of uncontrolled fury, just as she was about to launch herself on him again, Clive clenched his fist and took a swing at her. He caught her on the side of the chin with such an indelible force that you heard a bone crack, and she wheeled back from the impact.

He watched her put an arm out to break her fall. But instead the tip of her head hit the mantel.

Clive heard a great crack and she fell to the floor unconscious. A pool of blood came streaming out from behind her. She was certainly dead.

Clive panicked and paced around for some time before deciding to go through her things, looking for the $324 she withdrew from the bank.

He did not find it in her valise but rather found it in the pocket of the coat that she was still wearing.

Clive jumped when her body repositioned itself due to gravity.

He quickly tucked the money into his wallet and left.

He had no idea where he was going but he knew he had to leave.

His last thought was to go to Baxter's for a solution.

It was nighttime, and Tom and Baxter had just retired to bed.

They had a habit of staying up with the lights out and talking.

They spoke of selling Baxter's family home and getting a place in New York, close to Columbia University.

Baxter had not applied to any universities as he wanted to take a year off and sort things out before concentrating on his studies.

However, the truth was Baxter hadn't any idea which major to pursue.

They had just drifted off to sleep when they heard the noise of rock's hitting their window.

Baxter got up and looked out onto the lawn to see Clive Wills. He was looking directly at him.

It was at this moment that Baxter realized that he never mentioned the entire episode to Tom about Clive.

Baxter opened the window and told Clive to wait and that he would come down. Tom got up to see who it was, but it was too dark to see.

A wave of uncertainty came over Tom as Baxter told him that it was the boxer Clive whose match they watched during their crazy night together.

And without explanation, Baxter put on his robe and found his slippers and went downstairs. When Baxter left Tom walked to the front window only to get a glimpse of who was there. Clive didn't see Tom at the window as he was walking towards the door, hoping that Baxter would let him in.

The house was completely dark, but Baxter instinctively knew where everything was.

It was cold for a late August night and Baxter shivered due to the cold.

Baxter didn't let Clive enter but rather came outside.

"Hello Clive." said Baxter.

"I've got to get away and I want you to come with me."

Clive was breathing heavily while pacing in the yard. There was an uneasy sense of panic about him.

"Don't you have a wife?"

"She ain't in the picture no more." said Clive with a tinge of anger in his voice.

In the distance, there was police car sirens going off, which put Clive on edge.

The neighbors who lived below Clive and Dottie called the police when a spot of moisture first appeared on their ceiling. At first, the neighbors thought Dottie had flooded the bathroom but determined it was much more when the spot darkened, and a maroon color of red drops formed on the ceiling.

They thought it best to investigate.

They first knocked but got no answer. The door was unlocked and to their horror they saw Dottie's lifeless body illuminated by the city street lights.

They immediately called the police.

Baxter sensed the desperation in Clive and thought something was awry.

"This is so sudden Clive. I am in the middle of mourning. I had asked for some time but I was hoping months not days."

Clive grabbed at Baxter, jolting the young man into fear.

"Look, this is serious, can I crash here for a while?"

Baxter lied and told him that there were servants in the house, and it wouldn't be wise.

Clive thought again and concluded Baxter was correct as his picture would probably be in the paper for the murder of his wife and the servants would turn him in.

Baxter said that he would help but asked to follow his orders completely. He then told Clive that there is a transfer station in Harrison, New Jersey that is a transfer station with no outside passenger access. The police would not look for him there. There is the 491 late train to Manhattan. Baxter stressed that the 491 train will be leaving in about an hour and that Clive should be on it. He added that from Manhattan - Penn Station, to change to the Pennsylvania Line No. 159 to Washington DC. The last leg would be the 27 Train onto Atlanta, Georgia.

Clive lied and said he didn't have the money to get him there.

Baxter said that he would help but to go wait by the window.

Again, Clive pressed for Baxter to come with him and then he did something that he never thought he would ever do.

Clive kissed Baxter.

It was more of a peck but he thought it would suffice to show his intent, but Baxter still didn't return the sentiment.

"Come with me, please Baxter."

Without answering, Baxter instructed him to wait there.

When Baxter entered the house, Tom was there, at the top of the stairs, waiting. A nervous look was on his face.

"Baxter what is going on?"

But Baxter didn't answer, he just ran to his father's office and rambled through his father's desk pulling out a box which contained a large amount of money. He then search the desk drawers again, found an envelope and, ran back upstairs.

Tom was still waiting for him in the upstairs hallway. He looked confused. In desperation Tom asked "Are you leaving with him?" to which Baxter replied "Absolutely not."

Baxter scribbled down the train route numbers on a piece of paper then stuffed the money and the paper into the envelope. It barely fit as it was a large number of bills but he managed to seal it.

He then took the empty flask that Clive had given him and went to the front sitting room window and opened it.

He first threw the flask and then the envelope down to Clive.

The police sirens were getting louder.

"Hurry, you should catch the train and you don't have much time to get to the station. The train instructions are there and there is enough money for you to be okay."

Tom was behind him, but Baxter pulled him towards the window for Clive to see.

"I'm okay staying here. Goodbye Clive."

Tom was now in full view. Upon seeing Tom with Baxter, Clive knew the truth. A rage of betrayal surged over Clive like never before and he screamed out: "No! Don't do this to me!"

Soon lights in the neighbouring houses started to turn on, making Clive panic. He grabbed the flask and the envelope and disappeared into the night.

Baxter turned to Tom and took him by the hand and lead him back to bed.

He gently kissed Tom.

"Let's talk about this tomorrow. For now, I am tired and I am done counting my sins, Tom, I am with you and I love you."

The End.

Other books by Icon Empire Press:

Visit our website: www.gaybooks.info

Would You Mind? by Robert Joseph Greene

(ISBN 9781927124260)

Nate Lawson didn't know the kind of parents he had until he fell in love with another guy in high school. This wasn't just any guy, it was Mike Sarafin, the boy Nate had a crush on since the 8th Grade. Would You Mind? looks at those two boys, their families and their love for one another. Your family can surprise you sometime and give you the greatest gift of all, their love and acceptance.

Icon Empire Press

This High School Has Closets

(ISBN 9781927124048)

Sometimes coming out during high school just isn't an option. For Mark Thomas, finding out that he was gay falling in love, and dealing with becoming an adult, made it even tougher. High school is a challenge. "This High School Has Closets" is a story of two young teenagers falling in love during a difficult senior year.

The Gay Icon Classics Of The World (Revised Edition)

(ISBN 978-1-927124-43-7)

A wonderful collection of gay short fiction fables from around the world. The creation of these stories were based upon some cultural awareness of gay men in history and in some cultures where gay life is taboo. This is a must read for people who are interested in gaining an understanding of gays from different cultures and the human heart. Table of Contents 1. Introduction 2. The Journey and the Jewels – Saudi Arabia 3. And Cupid Also Loved – Rome 4. Haakon of Hearts – Sweden 5. The Wrong Voice Far Away – Egypt 6. Bantu's Song and the Soiled Loin Cloth – Côte d'Ivoire

7. The Five Bows of Shakespeare's Apprentice – Great Britain 8. The Three Wishes – Mexico 9. The Barton – France 10. The Love of Falleron and Ibsen – Greece 11. Halo's Golden Circle – Judea (Israel)